Thistle and Thyme

Presented with the
compliments of
The Bodley Head
1887-1987

Thistle and Thyme

Tales and Legends from Scotland

retold by

SORCHE NIC LEODHAS

THE BODLEY HEAD

LONDON SYDNEY

TORONTO

This book is for
Jenifer Jill Digby and
Maxine McFarland Digby
Ceud mìle fàilte!

The eighteen stories in this book
were originally published by
Holt, Rinehart and Winston,
New York,
in two volumes entitled
Heather and Broom and
Thistle and Thyme

The eight stories on pp.
31, 43, 69, 85, 115, 146, 168, 194
first published as *Heather and Broom*,
copyright © 1960 by
Leclaire G. Alger

The remaining ten stories,
first published as *Thistle and Thyme*,
copyright © 1962 by
Leclaire G. Alger

British Library Cataloguing in Publication Data
Nic Leodhas, Sorche
Thistle and thyme: stories and legends
from Scotland.
1. Tales – Scotland 2. Legends – Scotland
I. Title
398.2′09411 PZ8.1
ISBN 0-370-30681-3

Printed and bound in Finland
for The Bodley Head Ltd
9 Bow Street, London WC2E 7AL
by Werner Söderström Oy
This edition first published in Great Britain 1965
Reprinted 1975
Reprinted and bound in this format 1985

Introduction

Scotland has stories of so many different sorts that the richness of their variety is almost beyond believing. There are old, old legends which are as much like myths as they are like anything else. Then there are legends of the supernatural and of saints, which have come down to us in old monkish records. And there are the popular legends, which are sometimes sentimental and often very funny, and which were sometimes ballads in the beginning.

When someone tells you a Scottish story and you ask where it came from, he may say, 'I had it from my father, and he had it from his father.' But sometimes the answer will be, 'My father had it from a storyteller that came by one time.' Or 'There was an old bodach (fellow) that used to come by telling stories, and my grandmother had the tale from him.' These last will be the seanachie stories.

The first seanachies were the monks. As they were the only ones who knew how to write, they kept the records, and wrote down the ancient history of Scotland. They were not storytellers, but story collectors. There was as much fiction as fact in what they wrote, so the old manuscripts were mostly collections of stories.

The harpers learned some of the stories. They went about from one castle or manor to another with the old stories and with new ones that they made up themselves about stirring events which they heard about as they travelled. They did not tell their stories, but sang them to the music of the Gaelic harp which could be carried on the arm. They were called bards sometimes, but they were seanachies of a sort.

I do not know when the seanachies of the later times began to come along, but it was probably around 1600, for before that it was not easy for a man to leave his village and go wandering about. There were laws which made him stay in his own parish or on the estate to which he belonged. But about that time seanachies began to appear at fairs and at festive gatherings of the people. Some of them only told their stories but there were a few who sold them, printed on sheets of paper. Then they began to go about, not to the great houses, but to the small villages and lonely shielings (cottages) telling their stories for a meal and a night's lodging.

There were a few stories about clan chieftains which had an historical source, but these wandering seanachies suited their stories to the people to whom they were told, so they are cottage or household stories for the most part. And even the historical stories have in them, almost always, some sort of fairy person.

There were still seanachies going about during the 1800s. There were seanachies in Perthshire in 1830, and in Athole, and some of the counties of the northern and western Highlands in the 1850s. Some of the stories travelled far, for the people who heard them remembered them and told them again, carrying the stories along with them wherever they went. I have heard there was a seanachie in Nova Scotia as late as

1890. But I myself have never met one, and I think it is probable that cars, the cinema and radio put them out of business.

Another sort of Scottish story is the cottage tale, which somebody made up to amuse folk gathering around the fire on long winter evenings. There are usually fairy people of some kind in cottage stories. They are true folk tales and have been handed down almost as they were first told.

Some of the most interesting Scottish stories are the sgeulachdan (skale-ak-tan). The special thing about a sgeulachdan is that it is almost never written down. The composer of a sgeulachdan was (and still is, I have been reliably told) someone who had won some renown as a story-maker-and-teller among his friends and neighbours. And the sgeulachdan (which translated simply means tale) was almost always told as part of the entertainment at some sort of a ceilidh (kay-lee) or gathering, such as a wedding, a wake, a christening or the like. Sometimes they were told in impromptu rhyme, and almost always they pointed a moral, or had a theme suited to the occasion.

Gaelic folks have never been hard put to find a reason for a ceilidh. Weddings, or the announcement of an intention to wed, are the best and likely to produce the most merriment, but a christening is good, too, and so is the return of one who has been far and long away from home. No matter what brings folk together, you may be sure that there will be a grand feast spread, and the singing of old songs and ballads, the dancing of reels and most probably speeches to follow. But in the old days, the high point of the entertainment was the sgeulachdan.

The man who was going to tell it was always well

prepared. As soon as he received his bidding, or invitation, to the ceilidh, he knew that he'd be called upon to tell a tale. Why wouldn't he be, being famous for just that in all the countryside? So he'd be casting around in his mind for things to make it out of, and putting them together. And from maybe an idea he got from an old tale he'd heard, or from something that had happened to someone that he'd been told about, he made up his story. After he'd got it together, he changed it about and polished it and burnished it, until he was satisfied that it couldn't be bettered, and there was his sgeulachdan ready for telling.

There was a special art in the telling of it, too. When the story-maker-and-teller stood up before the company to tell it at last, he had a way of making it seem to fit the occasion even better. He did this by starting out with an introduction which he invented as he went along, telling what the ceilidh was for, and bringing in the names of the guests or guests of honour, and hinting at the things he was going to tell about. When he was well into the sgeulachdan, he'd begin to put in asides about this person or that, who was standing there listening, making the lasses blush and giggle, and the lads shuffle their feet awkwardly and look at each other with a wink or a grin, and setting the rest of the crowd roaring with laughter — until it was their turn to be the butt of the joke. Unless the sgeulachdan was a serious one, the telling of it could be a very hilarious affair.

Stories like those in this book are told, not written, but handed down from one storyteller to another. As there are no printed records of them, a writer can only come by them by hearing them told by someone who heard them himself. Considering this it is remarkable that they have come down to us with so many of the old Gaelic phrases, and so much of the cadence and intonation of the Gaelic intact.

The stories in this collection were all told to me long ago, and I have reconstructed them from a few notes and the echoes of their telling in my mind.

Contents

CONTENTS

The Laird's Lass and the Gobha's Son

———

AN OLD laird had a young daughter once and she was the pawkiest piece in all the world. Her father petted her and her mother cosseted her till the wonder of it was that she wasn't so spoiled that she couldn't be borne. What saved her from it was that she was so sunny and sweet by nature, and she had a naughty merry way about her that won all hearts. The only thing wrong with her was that when she set her heart on something she'd not give up till she got what it was she wanted.

Nobody minded so much while she was a wee thing, but when she was getting to be a young lady, that's when the trouble began.

She turned out better than anyone would have expected, considering all. You wouldn't have found a bonnier lass if you searched far and wide. But she was as stubborn as ever about having her own way.

Well, now that she was old enough the laird decided it was time to be finding a proper husband for her to wed, so he and her mother began to look about for a suitable lad.

It didn't take long for the lass to find out what they had in mind. She began to do a bit of looking around on her own. She hadn't the shade of a bit of luck at first. All the men who came to the castle were too fat or too thin or too short or too tall or else they were wed already. But she kept on looking just the same.

It was a good thing for her that she did, because one day as she stood at the window of her bedroom she saw the lad she could fancy in the courtyard below.

She called to her maid: 'Come quick to the window! Who is the lad down below?'

The maid came and looked. 'Och, 'tis only the son of the gobha that keeps the shop in the village. No doubt the laird sent for him about shoeing the new mare,' she said. And she went back to her work.

'How does it come that I ne'er saw him before?' asked the lass.

'The gobha's shop is not a place a young lady would be going to at all. Come away from the window now! Your mother would be in a fine fret could she see you acting so bold.'

And no doubt she was right, for the lass was hanging over the windowsill in a most unladylike way.

The lass came away as she was told, but she had made up her mind to go down to the village and get another look at the gobha's son.

She liked the jaunty swing to his kilt and she liked the way his yellow hair swept back from his brow and she had a good idea there'd be a lot of other things about him she'd be liking, could she be where she could get a better look at him.

She knew she wouldn't be let go if she asked, so she just went without asking. And to make sure nobody'd know her, she borrowed the dairymaid's Sunday frock and bonnet. She didn't ask for the loan of them either, but just took them away when nobody was around to see.

The gobha's shop was a dark old place but it wasn't

so dark that she couldn't see the gobha's son shoeing the laird's new mare.

His coat was off and his arms were bare and he had a great smudge of soot on his cheek, but she liked what she saw of him even better than before.

He was holding the mare's leg between his knees and fixing the new shoe on its hoof, so she waited till he finished. Then she stepped inside.

'Good day,' said she.

'Good day,' said he, looking up in surprise. And he gave her a great wide smile that fair turned her heart upside down.

So she gave him one as good in return. 'I'm from the castle,' said she. 'I just stopped in as I passed by to see how you were coming on with the mare.'

'I've two shoes on and two to go,' said he. 'Bide here a bit and I'll ride you up on her back when I'm done.'

'Och, no!' said the laird's daughter. 'I just stopped by. They'll be in a taking if I'm late coming home.'

Though he begged her to stay, she would not. So off she went.

He was not well pleased to see her go for he'd taken a terrible fancy to her and wanted to know her better. It was only after she was gone that he remembered he'd never asked her name.

When he took the mare back, he tried to find out which of the maids from the castle had been in the village that day. But there were maids galore in the castle and half a dozen or more had been in the village on one errand or another, so he got no satisfaction. He had to go home and hope he'd be seeing her soon again. Whoever she was and wherever she was, she'd taken his heart along with her.

The laird's daughter had come home and put the dairymaid's frock and bonnet back where she got them. After she made herself tidy, she went to find her father. She found him with her mother in the second-best parlour and she stood before them and said, 'You can just stop looking for a husband for me to wed because I've found the one I want myself.'

The laird laughed, for he thought it a joke she was making, but he soon found out it was not.

'I'm going to marry the gobha's son!' said she.

The laird flew into a terrible rage. But no matter what he said, it was all of no use. The lass had made up her mind, and he couldn't change it for her. And it was no use bothering the gobha's son about it, because he didn't even know who she was. He'd just tell the laird he'd never laid eyes on his daughter.

Well, the laird could only splutter and swear, and his lady could only sit and cry, and the lass was sent to bed without her supper. But the cook smuggled it up to her on a tray so that did her no harm at all.

The next morning the laird told her that she and her mother were going to Edinbro' in a week's time. And there she'd stay until she was safely wed to her second cousin twice-removed that he'd finally picked to be her husband. The cousin had asked for her hand before, but the laird had been putting him off in case someone better came along. But the way things were, the laird had decided he'd better take the cousin after all, and get his daughter wedded to a husband her mother and he had picked for her themselves.

'I'll go if I must,' said the lass. 'But you can tell my cousin that I'll not be marrying him. I've made up my mind to wed the gobha's son!'

The gobha's son was having his own troubles.

When the laird and his family came out of the church on the Sabbath morn, they passed by the gobha and his son at the gate. When they'd gone by, the gobha's son pulled at his father's arm.

'Who is the lass with the laird and his lady?' he asked his father.

His father turned and looked. 'Och, you ninny!' said he in disgust. 'Can you not see 'tis no lass at all? 'Tis a young lady, so it is! That's the laird's own daughter.'

The gobha's son had been building cloud-castles about the lass he'd thought was one of the castle maids, and now they all tumbled down. His heart was broken because he was so unlucky as to fall in love with the daughter of the laird.

Well, the days went by till it came to the one before the lass and her mother were to go to Edinbro'. The lass rose from her bed at break of dawn and dressed herself and tiptoed down the stairs. Since this was going to be her last day at home, she wanted to have a little time to be alone for it seemed that either the laird or her mother or else her maid was at her elbow ever since she'd told them she meant to wed the gobha's son.

The cook was in the kitchen as she passed through to the back door of the castle. The cook was picking something up from the floor.

'What have you there?' asked the lass.

' 'Tis a bairn's wee shoe,' said the cook. 'One of the laird's dogs fetched it in and dropped it on the floor just now as he went through. It must belong to one of the gardener's weans. 'Tis a bonny wee shoe and much too good for the likes of them,' she added with a sniff.

'Give it to me,' said the lass. 'I'll find the bairn that owns it.' She took the shoe and dropped it in her pocket.

Around the stables she went and through the kitchen garden to the lane that led to the gardener's house. Halfway there she came upon a wee small old man sitting on the bank at the side of the lane with his head in his hands. He was crying as if his heart would break. He was the smallest manikin ever she'd seen. He was no bigger than a bairn and indeed he looked so like a bairn, sitting there and weeping so sorely, that she sat down beside him and put her arms about him to comfort him. 'Do not greet so sore,' said she. 'Tell me your trouble and if I can I'll mend it.'

' 'Tis my shoe!' wept the wee man. 'I took it off to take out a stone that got in it, and a great rough dog snatched it from my hand and ran off with it. I cannot walk o'er the briars and brambles and the cruel sharp stones without my shoe and I'll ne'er get home today.'

'Well now!' said the lass, with a laugh. 'It seems I can mend your troubles easier than my own. Is this what you're weeping for?' And she put her hand in her pocket and took out the shoe she had taken from the cook.

'Och, aye!' cried the wee man. ' 'Tis my bonny wee shoe!' He caught it from her hand and put it on and, springing into the road, he danced for joy. But in a minute he was back, sitting on the bank beside her.

'Turnabout is only fair,' said he. 'What are your troubles? Happen I can mend them as you did mine.'

'Mine are past mending,' said the lass. 'For they're taking me to Edinbro' in the morn to wed my second cousin twice-removed. But I'll not do it. If I can't marry the gobha's son, I'll marry no man at all. I'll lay down and die before I wed another!'

'Och, aye!' said the wee man thoughtfully. 'So you want to marry the gobha's son. Does the gobha's son want to wed you?'

'He would if he knew me better,' the lass said.

'I could help you,' the manikin told her, 'but you might have to put up with a bit of inconvenience. You mightn't like it.'

'Then I'll thole it,' the lass said. 'I'd not be minding anything if it came right for me in the end.'

'Remember that,' said the wee man laughing, 'when the right time comes.'

Then he gave her two small things that looked like rowan berries, and told her to swallow them before she slept that night.

'You can leave the rest to me,' said he with a grin. 'You'll not be going to Edinbro' in the morn!'

When the night came, what with packing and getting ready for the next day's journey, all in the castle went to bed early, being tired out. The laird locked the door of his daughter's room lest the lass take it into her head to run away during the night.

Early the next morn, the maid came up with the lass's breakfast tray. Since the door was locked, she had to put the tray down and go and fetch the key from the laird's room.

'I'll come with you,' the lass's mother said to the maid. So she got the key from under the laird's pillow and unlocked the lass's door. When she opened the door and went in, she screamed and fainted away. The maid behind her looked to see why, and the tray dropped out of her hands. The laird heard the racket and came running. He rushed into the room, and there was his wife on the floor, and the maid, with the tray and the dishes and all at her feet, wringing her hands. He looked at the bed. His daughter wasn't there!

'She's flummoxed us!' said the laird. 'Where can she have gone to?'

He and the maid got the laird's wife into a chair and brought her to. The first thing she said was, 'Have you looked at the bed?'

'I have!' said the laird grimly. 'The pawky piece! She's got away. The bed's empty.'

'My love,' said his wife weakly. ' 'Tis not empty.'

The laird went over to the bed and his lady came with him. The bed was not empty, though his daughter was not in it.

In her place, with its head on the pillow and its forelegs on the silken coverlet, lay a wee white dog!

'What is that dog doing in my daughter's bed?' shouted the laird. 'Put the beastie out in the hall at once!' And he made to do it himself. But his wife caught his arm.

'I do not think it is a dog,' she said. 'I very much fear the wee dog is our daughter.'

'Havers!' the laird said angrily. 'Have you all gone daft?'

But they pointed out to him that the doggie was wearing the blue silk nightgown that her mother's own hands had put on her daughter last night. And hadn't the maid braided her young lady's hair and tied it with a blue satin ribbon? Well then, look at the wee dog's forelock all braided and tied the same. 'Twas plain to see that someone had put a spell on the lass and turned her into a dog.

'Nonsense!' said the laird in a rage. 'Are you telling me I do not know my daughter from a dog?' And he strode over to the bed. But when he leaned over to pluck the animal from the covers, it looked up at him. The laird looked back in horror, for he saw that the eyes were his daughter's own, and the grin on its face was uncommonly like his lass's own wide naughty smile. And around its neck was the golden chain with the locket he'd given her long ago, that she'd worn since he put it there.

But the laird would not admit it. 'Twas all a trick! So he made them search the room from corner to corner and in every cupboard and press. He looked up the chimney himself and got himself covered with smuts, but all he saw was the blue sky above the chimney pot. She was not in the room. She couldn't have got out of the windows. She couldn't have gone through the door, for he'd had the key to it. So it all came to this—the wee dog in the bed was his daughter.

He went over to have another look and as he bent down, the little dog chuckled with his daughter's own pleased chuckle and patted him on the cheek just as his daughter used to do. That settled it.

'Och, you wee rascal!' said the laird, never being able to find it in his heart to be angry with his daughter. 'Now what are we to do?' There was one thing that was certain and sure. They'd not be going to Edinbro' that day. So a messenger was sent to the second cousin twice-removed, to tell him that he needn't be expecting them. The servants were told the lass was down in bed with some sort of an illness, and nobody but her maid was to be let come into the room lest they catch it. That was enough to keep them all away.

The laird had his own physician come from Edinbro' though his wife told him 'twould do no good at all. He made the man promise not to tell what he saw, then took him into his daughter's room. The doctor looked and shook his head. Then he looked at the dog again and rubbed his eyes. ' 'Tis strange!' he muttered. 'I do not see a young lady. I see naught but a wee white dog.'

'You see a dog because there is a dog!' shouted the laird.

' 'Tis an optical delusion! Begging your laird-ship's pardon, your lairdship's daughter is not a dog,' insisted the doctor.

' 'Tis my daughter,' the laird roared. 'And she is a dog. So be off with you!'

Well, the maid and his wife were right. The doctor was no use at all. He went back to Edinbro' and wrote a learned paper called '*Remarkable Manifestation of Hallucination in A————shire*,' which was read by learned societies all over the world, but didn't help the laird at all.

Then the maid suggested they send for an old wife she'd heard of. The old woman came with herbs and powders, but all she could do was tell them the lass had been bewitched. How to take the spell off, she didn't know at all.

The laird tried a gipsy woman next, but all that got him was the loss of a silver comb she must have slipped into her pocket. It wasn't missed until after she'd gone away.

The laird was fair distracted, her ladyship took to her bed, and the maid went about in tears from morn till night. All the servants in the castle said it must be a mortal illness the young lady had on her and they tippy-toed and grieved as they went about their work.

The maids carried the news to the village, and the

gobha's son soon heard all about it. If he thought his
heart was broken before, it was twice as bad when he
thought the laird's daughter might be about to die.
For if she were living, at least he'd have a chance to
lay his eyes on her now and again. He felt he couldn't
be expected to bear it.

He was hammering away at a bit of metal his father
had told him to make a brace of, not even noticing the
iron had gone cold, when a shadow fell across the door.
He looked up and there was the strangest sight he'd
ever seen in his life. A wee bit of a man was there, all
dressed in green from his neck to his heels, and his
shoes and his cap were red. He was mounted on a
horse so small it could have stood under the belly of
any horse the gobha's son had ever seen before, but
it was the right size for the wee man in green.

The gobha's son stared, while the wee man got down
from his horse and led it into the shop.

'Gobha,' said the wee man. 'Can you shoe my
horse?'

'I'm not the gobha,' said the lad. 'I'm the gobha's
son and I can shoe your horse. 'Twill take me a while,
for I've ne'er shod a beast so small before and I've no
notion of the size the shoes must be.'

' 'Tis no matter,' said the wee man. 'I've time galore.
I'll sit and gab a bit with you till the task is done.'

So he made himself comfortable in a corner beyond
the forge, and crossing his knees with an easy air, he
started to talk to the gobha's son.

It was plain to see that the lad was in no mood for
talking. The wee man said the weather had been fine
for the time of the year. The lad said only, 'Aye. Is
it?'

Then the man in green said the fishing was good,

he'd heard. To that the lad said happen it was. He wouldn't be knowing.

Then the manikin tried him on the fair in the market town over the hill, but the gobha's son only sighed and said nothing at all.

It was taking a long time, as he said it would, for the horse's hooves were small beyond believing. Shoe after shoe had to be thrown back because they were all too big. But at last he got a set that would fit, and putting the horse where the light fell best, he started to put the horseshoes on its feet.

I'll get you talking yet, my lad, the wee man said to himself.

So, when the gobha's son started to put the shoe on the wee nag's foot, the manikin said, 'Have you e'er seen the bonny daughter of the laird up at the castle?'

The gobha's son jumped as if he'd been stuck with a pin. But all he said was, 'Aye.'

The wee man waited until the lad finished putting the first shoe on. When he picked up the second leg and started to fix the second shoe to the hoof, the wee man asked, 'Has anyone told you that she's mortal ill?'

The gobha's son gave a great big sigh, but all he said was, 'Aye.'

He finished with that shoe and went round to the other side of the wee horse. When he looked to be well started on the third shoe, the man in green asked, 'Have you no been up to the castle to ask about the laird's bonny daughter?'

The gobha's son shot him a glowing look. 'Nay,' said he.

That took care of the chatting between the two until the horse was nearly shod. As he was about to fix the last nail in the last of the shoes, the man in green said, 'Would you be knowing what ails the bonny young lady?'

The gobha's son waited until he had finished his work and the horse stood with shoes on all four feet. Then he turned to the wee man and he said, 'Nay!' He threw the hammer he'd been using aside and told the wee man, 'There's your horse all shod and well shod. Now will you take it and yourself away and leave me in peace?'

The wee man stayed where he was. 'Not yet!' said he with a grin. 'Why do you not go up to the castle and cure the laird's bonny daughter yourself?'

'Cure her!' shouted the gobha's son. 'I'd lay down my life to cure her, the bonny young thing.' And he asked the wee man furiously, 'How could the likes of me do any good when they've had the gipsy woman with her spells, and the old wife with her herbs and simples, and the best physician come all the way from Edinbro', and not one of them could set her on her feet again?'

'Whisht, lad!' the manikin scolded. 'Would you have all the village running to see what the matter can be? To be sure, they couldn't help her. But I know a way you could cure her. If you'd want to.'

As soon as the gobha's son heard that, he was at the wee man to tell him, so that he could run to the castle at once and cure the laird's daughter of her illness.

'Answer me this first,' the green manikin said. 'Would you like to wed the bonny young lady?'

'Are you daft?' groaned the lad. 'Who ever heard of a gobha's son wedding the daughter of a laird?'

' 'Tis not what I asked you,' said the wee man. 'Look, lad! *Would you like to wed her?*'

'Before I'd wed with anyone else, I'd just lay down and die!' cried the gobha's son.

' 'Tis just what the laird's daughter said about yourself,' said the wee man with a satisfied grin. 'So, since you are both of the same mind, I'll help you!' Then the wee green man told the gohba's son what he and the lass had been up to.

'Och, nay!' said the lad. ' 'Tis beyond believing.'

'It all started because she made up her mind to wed the gobha's son,' said the manikin. 'So let's you and me be finishing it!'

The wee man gave him two wee things, like rowan berries, as like the ones he'd given the lass as they could be.

'Here's the cure for what ails her,' he told the gobha's son.

The lad was all for rushing off to the castle at once, but the wee man held him back.

'Will you be going up to the castle the way you are with your leather apron and soot from the forge all over you?' he scolded. 'Och, they'd run you off the place e'er you got the first word in. Tidy yourself first, lad!'

So the lad went and cleaned himself up and got into his Sunday clothes, and a fine figure he was, to be sure. 'Twas no wonder the laird's daughter had set her heart upon him!

'Go with my blessing,' said the wee man. 'But remember! Don't cure the lass till the laird has given his promise that you can wed her.'

'That I'll not!' said the gobha's son. He squared his shoulders, and off he marched to the castle.

The wee man got on his wee horse's back and where he rode to, nobody knows.

Things at the castle were in a terrible state. The laird was at his wits' end. The laird's wife and the castle servants had wept till the walls of the castle were damp with the moisture from their tears. The laird's daughter was getting tired of being a dog, and beginning to fear that she'd ne'er be anything else for the rest of her life. She had snapped at the laird's hand that morning because she was cross with him for not letting her wed the gobha's son in the first place. 'Twas a weary day for the old laird.

The gobha's son walked up to the front door and asked to see the laird. He had such a masterful way with him the servants let him in at once. In no time at all there he was, face to face with the laird.

The laird had left his manners off for the time. 'Well, who are you and what do you want?' he asked with a frown.

'I'm the gobha's son,' said the lad. When the laird heard who it was, he jumped from his chair and started for the lad, ready to throw him out with his own two hands. Because it was the gobha's son who was at the bottom of all the trouble.

The gobha's son sidestepped the laird and said quickly, 'And I've come to cure your daughter.'

Och, now! That made a difference. Where the laird had been all wrath and scowls, he was now all smiles. He caught the lad by the arm and said, 'A hundred thousand welcomes! Come, let's be going to her then.'

'Nay,' said the lad. 'I must know first what I'll get for it.'

'Do not let that fash you,' the laird said eagerly. 'Och, I'll give you a whole big bag of gold. Or two if you like. Come. Let's be at it!'

' 'Tis not gold I want,' said the lad.

'What is it, then?' the laird asked impatiently.

'Your leave to marry your daughter,' said the lad as bold as brass.

'Nay!' thundered the laird. 'That you shan't have.'

'Then I'll bid you good day,' said the gobha's son, and started for the door.

But he never got there. The laird was beside him before he laid his hand on the door knob.

What could the poor old laird do? He had to give in and he knew it. So he did.

'You can have her,' said the laird to the gobha's son.

The wee dog jumped from the bed and ran up to the gobha's son the minute he and the laird came into the room. The lad took the berries from his pocket and popped them into her mouth and she swallowed them down. Before you could say, 'two two's,' there stood the laird's daughter in the wee dog's place!

She took the lad's hand in her own and she turned to the laird and said, 'I'm going to wed the gobha's son.'

'Wed him then!' said the laird, not too unhappy about it since he'd got his lass back again. 'But you'd better go and tell your mother and the maids, so they can stop crying if you want the castle dried out by the time of your wedding.'

So the pawky lass got her way in the end and married the gobha's son. The laird was not ill pleased for he found his son-in-law as likeable a body as any he'd ever found. So he made him steward of his estates and a good one the lad was, too. So it all ended well and that's all there is to tell about the laird's daughter and the gobha's son.

The Gay Goss-Hawk

THERE WAS once a young English lady of very high degree. She had a father and seven brothers and a stepmother whom her father had married but lately. The father and her seven brothers loved her well enough, but the stepmother had no liking for her, being envious because the lady was young and good and beautiful, and the stepmother was none of the three. So the poor young English lady was not happy at home, for her stepmother lost no chance of making sure that she wouldn't be.

Well, there came a time when the English king called together all his court, and the young lady was there too, with all her family. And there she met a gay Scottish laird, who was so gentle and kind that she loved him without half trying and he loved her the same.

Well, since she loved him and he loved her they plighted their troth and promised to wed. As a pledge of love he gave her the gold ring from his finger, and she gave him a blue silken bow from her dress, tied in a true love knot.

The Scottish laird went to her father to ask for the lady's hand in marriage. But the father wouldn't have it at all, for he and her seven brothers had planned to marry her off to an old English lord who was very wealthy, and who also had the ear of the

English king ready to listen to whatever he liked to say.

The Scottish laird had plenty of gold and a house and land. He had a thousand good men of his clan to serve him in his need. But the lady's father scorned the Scots, as a proud, wild, stiff-necked race, and he told the laird he'd have none of him to be his son-in-law.

Then the stepmother said the lovers would be meeting, since they were at the king's court together, so to prevent it her father carried her off to his own castle far away. After she had gone, the Scottish laird had no pleasure at the king's court, so he packed up and went back to his own castle in the North country.

The only thing that pleased him there was a gay goss-hawk that he had. He soon grew fond of it, for it sang to him merrily when he was sad. And it went with him wherever he went and was his faithful companion. It would perch on his knee when he sat, or sit by his plate when he ate, or ride on his wrist as he went about his lands. It was a very intelligent bird, and had learned to know the laird so well that it understood all that he said to it.

But nothing could comfort the laird for the loss of his love. He grew as wan and pale in his castle as the lady did in hers.

At last the laird sat down and wrote a letter to his love, and in it, he told her to come to him soon or he would surely die. He told the goss-hawk that he must carry the letter to England and give it to the young English lady.

'Though you've never laid eyes upon her,' he said to the goss-hawk, 'you'll know her from all the rest, for she is the fairest lady of all in the length and breadth of the land.'

Then the laird told the bird the way he was to go, to find the lady's father's castle. When the goss-hawk got there he was to sit in the birch tree that stood by the door of the lady's bower, and when the lady came out with her maidens to go to church then he should sing so that the lady would notice him. If she stopped and came to the tree the goss-hawk could give her the letter.

The laird hung the true love knot the lady had given him about the goss-hawk's neck, so she'd know who was sending him to her.

The bird took the letter in its beak and stretched its wings out wide, and off it flew to the English castle.

When the goss-hawk came to the castle of the English lady's father he sat himself down upon a branch of the birch tree by the lady's bower that the laird had told him about. The letter he tucked under his wing to hide it away. By-and-by out comes the lady to church and all her maidens along with her. Right merrily did the goss-hawk sing, then, and the lady turned her head and looked back at him. When she saw the blue true love's knot about the bird's neck she knew who had sent him there, so she told her maidens to be walking on and she'd come to them a little later. So off they went without her and never turned to look back at her.

Back she went to the gay goss-hawk and bade him sing again. And first he sang a merry song and then he sang a sad one, and then he took the letter from under his wing and gave it to the fair English lady, for he knew that she was the one his master had told him about.

The lady unfolded the letter and began to read it. First she turned pale as a white rose and then she turned rosy as a red one, and when she finished she read it all again.

She wrote a letter to tell the laird to bake his bridal bread and to brew his bridal ale, because before either of them had a chance to grow stale she'd be at St Mary's church to meet him.

The goss-hawk took the letter and off and away he flew, and he never stopped for bite nor for sup till he'd laid the letter safe in the hand of the young Scottish laird.

When the bird was gone the lady sat long, to think what she was to do. Then she rose and went up to her bedchamber and laid herself down on her bed. Her maidens came seeking her, for it troubled them that she had not come to them at the church, and they found her lying there.

'Go fetch my father quickly,' she said, 'for I feel ill and I think I'm about to die!'

The maidens ran for her father and told him what she had said. He came and stood at her bedside, and she looked at him. 'Father,' said she, 'before I die will you grant one wish to me?'

'Do not ask for your Scottish laird,' her father said with a frown. 'Anything else I will promise to you, whatever it may be. But rather than see you wedded to yon proud Scottish laird I'd see you lying dead!'

'Well then,' said the lady, 'should I die, will you give me your promise true that my seven brothers shall carry me to Scotland to be buried? And when they come to the first church there let them stop and have the Mass sung over me. And when they come to the second church let them have the church bells tolled for me. But when they come to St Mary's church, they must set me down in the churchyard and wait there till the night.'

Her father promised all that she asked, and then he went away. In the dead of the night, when all in the castle were asleep and her old nurse dozing by the fire, the lady got up from her bed. She mixed herself a sleeping draught, and when it was mixed she drank it down, and then she slipped back into her bed.

At dawn of day the old nurse awoke, and there was her fair young lady lying so still and white that anyone would be sure she was dead. She roused all the castle and told them that the lady had died in her sleep. Her father came and her seven brothers came, and they all stood grieving about the lady's bed. Then came her stepmother and stood looking at her. 'We'll make sure she is dead then,' said the stepmother.

First she sent for a sharp silver pin, and when it was brought to her, she took it in her hand and stuck it into the lady's white arm. But the lady never blinked nor moved at all when the pin went in. Then the stepmother sent for a pan of hot, boiling wax, and when it came she dropped three drops of it upon the lady's white, white breast. But the lady did not sigh, nor did she flinch, but she lay there with no sign of life.

Then her seven brothers made a bier, and they made it all of oaken boughs. They covered it over with silver cloth, as was fitting for a lady of such high degree.

Her maidens took white velvet and made her a white velvet cap and a white velvet coverlet for her bier, and with every stitch they took, they sewed on a little silver bell.

When all was ready her maidens washed and dressed her, and they combed her long golden hair. They took her from her bed and they laid her on the silver bier, and upon her head they set the velvet cap, and they laid the velvet coverlet over her.

Then her seven brothers took up the bier, and all the little silver bells rang sweetly as they carried her away to Scotland.

When they came to the first church the seven brothers set the bier down, and there they had the Mass sung over her. At the second church they stopped again, and there her seven brothers had the church bells rung for her.

But the third Scottish church was St Mary's church. The seven brothers carried the bier into the churchyard, for there they were to wait until the night. But when they came in up sprang a hundred spearmen, and out from the midst of them stepped the young Scottish laird. He bade the seven brothers to set down the lady's bier, that he might look upon her face. He took her by the hand and up she rose at once, and smiled upon him lovingly. She set herself among the spearmen, with her true love by her side, and the little silver bells upon her velvet cap chimed merrily together all the while.

'Go home! My seven brothers, go home!' she said, 'for you've fetched me where I want to be!'

Then her seven brothers said, as they turned to go, 'Shame to you that left your father to grieve at home because he thought you were dead!'

'Take my love to my father,' she told them then, 'though he said he'd rather I were lying dead than married to my Scottish laird. But I send no love to my cruel stepmother for the sharp silver pin she stuck me with and the hot, boiling wax she burned me with, for to her I wish nothing but woe!'

Then she rode off gaily beside her Scottish laird and the next day they were wed. And wherever they went, there went the goss-hawk, too, that had brought them together when they were parted. And happy they were, for all their troubles, like this story, had come to an end.

Saint Cuddy and the Grey Geese

THERE WAS once a good saint at Mulross and his name was Saint Cuddy. If folks who have the notion they know better, tell you it was Cuthbert, don't you be believing them, for the folks of his own place always called him Cuddy and if they don't know, who does? It was this saint who had a great knowledge of birds and their ways and the manners of all wild things in the air or on the land or in the sea. The fame of his knowledge spread far from his own land to others in distant places. Great folks came to him to ask him things they didn't know themselves about the birds and the beasts. Saint Cuddy was a great one for tramping around the countryside and often even by night he'd be stravaging over the hills or along the shore, peeping into this and poking into that and inspecting and examining to find out what the wild creatures were up to.

The birds were what he liked best. 'Twas a marvel what he could do with them. He had such a way with the eider ducks that they're still remarkably tame. Folks still call them Cuddy's ducks. Loving the birds so dearly and knowing them so well, it is no wonder that when he got to Heaven they gave the flying creatures over to him, so he's the saint that's protector of the birds.

It wasn't just the birds Saint Cuddy kept an eye on.

He looked after people, too. When he was at home in his monastery, there was always a line of poor folks coming up the road to ask for help. Never a one of them went away empty-handed, and the kind word and the bit of good plain advice he gave them did them more good than the bundle of food they carried away, and they went home happier and wiser than they came.

The kind words were for those that deserved them. Whenever he came across anyone that was doing anything he shouldn't be doing, he had a whiplash to his tongue that could give a rare thrashing. And Saint Cuddy never held back from using it when he thought it was needed.

Well, being a great traveller, there wasn't much that went on that didn't come under his eye. What he didn't see for himself, he was bound to hear about, for someone was sure to tell him. So, one way or another he learned about the greedy old wife.

This old wife lived by her lone on her tidy farm, having neither husband nor bairn to keep her company. Her cow was sonsie, her sheep were fat, her henyard was a treat for the eye to see. But she was never one to share what she had. She was so greedy and close-fisted she was a scandal to all who knew her.

She had a crafty way of getting out of giving anything away. When poor folks came begging she'd tell them, 'Och, now! 'Tis terrible sorry I am! I'd give you somewhat sure but I've got a sluagh of poor kin and I've got to save whate'er I can spare for them.'

Then, when her poor relations came and asked her for help, she'd say, 'Well, now, I'd give and gladly if I could. But more than what I need for myself must

go to the poor, for they're worse off than yourself.'
That way neither the poor nor her poor relations got
a thing and she could keep all she had for herself.

When Saint Cuddy heard what was going on he
didn't like it at all, so off he went to have a talk with
the old wife herself.

Now it happened that she had a fine flock of geese
that she'd raised. She was mortal proud of them and
fed them and tended them well till they were fat
enough to drive to market to sell.

It was market day when Saint Cuddy came along
and met her on the road driving her great grey geese
before her. There were twelve of them and every one
so big and fine and fat it would make your mouth
water to look at them, and think what they'd be like
lying roasted on a platter!

Saint Cuddy was a very large man, and the way was
narrow. He stood in the middle of it and he filled it
up so that she couldn't get by on one side or the other.

'Good day to you, old wife,' said the saint. ' 'Tis
a fine lot of geese you've got there!'

'Fine or not,' said the old wife, 'I'll be troubling
you to move over so that I can get by with my geese.'

'Och, come now,' Saint Cuddy said pleasant-like.
'The morn's early yet. Hold a bit and the two of us
will be having a bit of gab.'

The old wife didn't know Saint Cuddy at all for
she'd never laid eyes on him before. But she wouldn't
have cared if she had.

'Get over, old bodach!' she ordered angrily, 'and
leave me and my geese go by.'

But Saint Cuddy moved not so much as an inch.
On the contrary, he sort of spread himself out further
over the road.

'Och, now, be easy,' he said in a soothering sort of a voice. 'Happen I can do you a good turn, woman.'

'The best turn you could do me would be to get on your way,' said the old wife. She was as cross now as two crossed sticks.

Saint Cuddy could see well that folks had been telling no lies about the old wife, but he was willing to give her a chance.

'They tell me you've been saving a goose for your poor kin over at Mulross,' said he. ' 'Tis on my way to Mulross I am myself. I'll just be taking it along with me and save you the trouble for the journey.'

'A goose for my poor kin indeed!' the old wife cried with scorn. 'If my kin were as careful and thrifty as me they'd have a goose of their own.'

'Och, well! Maybe so, maybe so,' the good saint agreed. 'But what of the one that I hear you've been setting by for the poor? We've a wheen of poor folk over at Mulross. How about me taking yon fat one along with me for them? Then you'll have done with that.' And he pointed his finger at the best goose of the lot.

The old woman flew into a rage. 'Not my kin nor the poor nor anyone else shall ever have one of my geese,' she shouted. 'As sure as I stand in this place. So be on your way, you blethering old man!' And she raised the stick she was driving the geese with and made as if to rush at the saint to drive him away.

Saint Cuddy raised his hand and thundered out in a mighty voice, 'As sure as you stand in this place, old wife? Then stand in this place you shall! And the geese you would not part with, for love of kin or charity to the poor, shall keep you company!'

And true it was. For where she stood she stayed.

41

She and her twelve fat grey geese had all turned into grey stones.

And if you should be coming along from Mulross towards the sea, you can see them for yourself. Twelve round grey stones in a line and a bigger one behind them just where the road makes a bend to get round them.

When the auld wife didn't come back, the poor relations got her farm. Now that they had a bit of gear of their own, they were as thrifty as anybody needs to be. But they were always good to the poor, for they remembered what it was like when they were poor themselves.

If you are thinking 'twas a hard thing that the grey geese should share the old wife's fate, remember they were all headed for market and if she'd got them there, they'd all soon have been roasted and eaten up. So no doubt the geese were well content with the way things turned out, and Saint Cuddy had done the very best thing for them after all.

The Lairdie with the Heart of Gold

THERE ONCE was a young Scottish lairdie that folks all said had a heart of gold. That was because he could not bear the sight of anybody in trouble without trying to do something to help them. He was that good-natured and open-handed, his like would be hard to find.

He was a wee lad when his mother died, and his father, the old laird, never got over her death. He sent the laddie to live with a connection of the family in the North country, for the son took after the mother so much that the old laird could not look upon his face without sorrow.

Well, the lad grew up, and by and by the old laird died, so they sent for the young lairdie to come back and take over the estates. When he did he was sorry he'd come, for the old laird had let everything go to rack and ruin whilst he shut himself up into his study and read his books and broke his heart over losing his wife.

When the notary read out the list of what was coming to the young laird it sounded grand enough. There was a lot of land, and a village with a kirk, and some farms here and there, and a grand park with deer in it. And, of course, there was the castle.

But when the lairdie rode about looking at what his father had left him, there was another side to the story. The land was there, right enough, but most of it had gone wild. Only two or three of the farms were being kept up proper, and the rest weren't worth the name. Most of the houses in the village were tumble-down, and as for the kirk, it looked noble enough outside, but inside it was fitter to use for a barn than for worship and it had a big hole in the roof. The deer in the park were the only things that the lairdie took any comfort in, for they were sleek and friendly, and nothing else he'd seen that day, human or not, had been either the one or the other.

And when he got back to the castle and gave it a good look over, he saw that it was as bad as all the rest. The only thing good about it was the old family servants, who loved him and tried to make him comfortable.

But it wasn't much wonder he wished he'd stayed away.

Well, half a dozen years went by, and things were no worse, for they couldn't be, but certainly little better. Every quarter day, when rents were due, 'twas always the same. Some of the tenants were honest, but couldn't pay because they had had ill luck. And some of them who were able to pay were dishonest, and put on a meeching look and pretended they didn't have any money either. Only the two or three good farmers paid up regularly and in full. So what the lairdie collected was hardly more than enough to keep bannocks and cheese on the table. But the lairdie was so goodhearted that he believed them all, and felt sorry for them.

He might have had more for himself if he'd turned the servants off, but they were all getting along in years and he was afraid they'd never find new places.

Besides, he loved them and they loved him, although about all they got out of it was a roof over their heads and as good to eat as he got—which wasn't any too much. There was a mortal lot of them, so the young laird worrited himself a good bit about how he'd take care of them all.

One winter's quarter day the lairdie came back in the gloaming from gathering rents all day, which was something he had to do himself, for if he had waited for them to be brought to him he'd have had a long, long wait. All he had got was excuses and promises, with barely enough money to tide him over until the next quarter day. He was that disheartened that he didn't know what to do. He'd left his horse at home because he didn't like to take the poor beast out all day in the bad wintry weather, so he plodded along on foot in the dusk with his head down against the snow and the wind.

There was a fork in the road where half of it went down to the mill beyond and the other half went up the hill to the castle. There at the place where the roads parted he saw what he took to be a heap of bairns' toys by the roadside, with a lot of poppets beside them. He couldn't see so well with the dark closing in, but when he got up to them he gave them another look. Then he saw the pile wasn't toys at all! Nor were the other things poppets, for they were all as alive and breathing as he was himself!

It was a whole lot of brownies, and the heap of things were their wee sticks of furniture.

'Well!' exclaimed the lairdie. 'What is it you're doing here, out in the wind and the snow and the cold?'

Then one of the brownies stepped out from the

rest. 'I'm Lachie Tosh,' said he, 'and this is my wife
and our seven sons and their wives, with each their
seven sons and their sons' wives and their bairns and
all. I'm the head of our *sept* of our clan,' said he, 'and
we're flitting.'

The lairdie bent down and politely took the hand
the wee man offered him.

'Where are you flitting to?' he asked.

'We're flitting from the mill,' Lachie Tosh told
him, 'and it's bitter hard that we should be made to.
The Toshes have always lived at the mill since time
began. My father, and his father, and his father's
father, and all our fathers before them have been mill
brownies. But the miller's wife died, and now he has
brought a new wife from the town and she'll have
naught to do with the brownies!'

'She says there are no brownies!' cried one of the
clan.

'She says we are just great brown rats!' shrieked
another.

Then they all began shouting at one and the same
time.

'She says that we steal the meal!'

'That we nibble holes in the cheese!'

'That we take the eggs from the nests!'

'That we skim the cream from the milk!'

'She brought in a great cruel cat to fright our bairns!'

'And two fierce dogs to chase us away from the
corn!'

'Whisht!' shouted Lachie Tosh and he held up a
hand. At once the babble stopped. 'So that's why
we're flitting,' said the brownie.

'Och aye!' said the lairdie. 'I can see that well. But
where will you be going now?'

46

'Well,' said Lachie Tosh, 'that's what we're doing here. We stopped to talk it over. But they've all been havering for an hour gone, and not yet picked a place.'

The laird was sore troubled by the brownies' plight. 'The castle has little to offer you,' he said, 'but you'd be warm and dry there anyway. The servants are an old-fashioned sort and I doubt not you'd be welcome. The cook has a cat, 'tis true, but she's a comfortable purring sort of a beastie and doesn't even trouble the mice. As for my two dogs, they would be no trouble to you, for they are that friendly they sport about the garden with the hares and do them no harm at all. Would you like to come with me to the castle?'

'Aye, that would we!' said Lachie Tosh.

But the lairdie thought he'd best give them a word of warning. 'You'll find we have not much to do with, but what we have we'll gladly share. There'll be porridge and milk, and happen a bannock and some cheese, too. Whatever there is you're welcome to it.'

'Say no more!' cried Lachie Tosh. 'Come all!'

The brownie men picked up their wee bits of furniture, and the brownie women took up their bundles and some of their smaller bairns, and up they all trooped after the laird to the castle.

The housekeeper met them in the hall, for she had been keeping an eye out for the lairdie. What with the dark coming on and him out so late she was near troubled to death.

When he opened the door and led the brownie folk in, she stood, dumbstruck, in her tracks.

'Mistress MacIvor,' the lairdie said to her, 'I've brought you the brownies o' the mill. They've been turned out by the miller's new, townbred wife, and have no place to shelter themselves in.'

The housekeeper found her tongue at that. 'Och, the poor wee things!' she cried. 'Come in! Come in all! Come in to the fire and give yourselves a warming.'

'Will ye have room for us all?' asked Lachie Tosh. 'We're wee, but there's awful many of us.'

'Is it room, he asks?' demanded the housekeeper. 'In this great place, with the few of us rattling about in it? Och, you'll be doing us a favour, helping to fill it up so it don't feel so empty-like!'

Lachie Tosh was well pleased with that and said so gratefully, and in no time at all the brownies were settled into the castle as if they'd always been there.

The cat and the dogs made no trouble at all. Indeed the cat seemed to think that the brownie weans were kittens of a sort, for she cuddled them and washed their faces and hands and purred them to sleep before the fire. As for the laird's dogs, they acted as if their lives had ne'er been complete till the brownies came.

The servants liked the brownies' cheerful chatter and their pleasant faces, and on the whole it was agreed that the castle was a better place since the brownies came. The candles burned brighter, the fires blazed higher and took less fuel to do it. The hens laid more eggs, the meal sack seemed to grow heavier instead of lighter each day, and there was more cream to the milk the cows gave. There seemed to be more food for the table instead of less, with all the extra mouths to be filled, so all were contented.

But no, not all. Lachie Tosh would go out every morn and be gone for a long time. When he came back the frown on his brow reached down to his rosy old cheeks and the corners of his mouth drooped down farther each day. And as for the laird, his nice young face grew longer and sadder day by day.

When the brownies had been in the castle a little above a month the lairdie sat in his study one day over his account books. The study was a cheerful place now, for the brownie women had everything as neat as a silver pin, and a big fire burned in the fireplace. But the laird's face was far from cheerful because he was trying to balance his accounts, and with so much paid out and so little paid in he couldn't do it.

Lachie Tosh came in and climbed up into a chair facing the laird. The laird laid his pen down, for he saw the brownie had come to talk to him.

'Lairdie,' said the brownie. 'I've something to say that happen you won't be liking.'

'Och, Lachie,' the laird said, 'there's naught you could say I'd take amiss.'

'Well, 'tis my way to speak plain, so speak plain I will!' said Lachie. 'I do not like the way things is going on here.'

'That is what I feared,' the laird said sadly. 'And now you'll be wanting to go away no doubt? Well, the castle is but a poor place and I cannot say I blame you. But it's glad we've been to have you here, and we'll all be sorry to see you go.'

'Och, nay!' said the brownie indignantly. 'You've read my meaning wrong! We're all as snug here as e'er we could hope to be. We're the castle brownies now! We're settled here to stay.'

'I'm happy to hear it,' said the laird with relief.

'It's things outside the castle is wrong,' said Lachie earnestly. ' "Wilful waste makes woeful want." That's where the trouble lies, lairdie!'

49

'I know it,' said the laird. 'I know it well.'

'And another thing,' said Lachie, 'butter and brawn in the cottage and bannocks and cheese in the castle is not right and never will be!'

'But how can the cottagers have butter and meat when they can't even pay their rents? There aren't many of them who can find money for things like that.'

'More than you know!' said Lachie.

'But how would they come by the money?' the laird insisted. 'They've told me often that they can't make ends meet.'

'They get the money by not paying their rent,' said Lachie. 'That's how!'

The laird looked at Lachie Tosh, and Lachie looked right back at him.

'I've been going round and about,' said Lachie. 'A wee person like me sees more than sees him. I know who has money laid by that hasn't paid their rent since the old laird's time. And the laziness and thriftlessness and shiftlessness I've seen makes the blood of me boil with rage. I'd best say no more about it!'

'No doubt you're right, Lachie,' said the laird. 'But what am I to do? I've thought till my head swims and I can't find a way to set things right.'

'It's the heart of gold of you,' said Lachie gently. 'You trust everybody and you believe every tale they tell you. You're too good to folks. Lairdie, what you need is a factor!'

'I'd have one if I could pay him,' said the laird. 'Someone who knows how to go about managing an estate would do much better than me. And well do I know it! How could I ever pay a factor?'

'How about me?' asked Lachie. 'I'll take it on if you like.'

The laird sat up in his chair and stared at the brownie. 'You, Lachie!' he exclaimed.

'Why not me?' asked Lachie. 'Me and the help I'd get from my sons, and my son's sons and the rest. 'Twould take a sharp rascal to be getting the better of all of us. 'Twould now!'

The laird looked troubled. 'I wouldn't want you to be hard on the folks whose luck has been lacking,' he said doubtfully.

'Those that deserve good will get it,' said Lachie firmly, 'and those that don't won't. And you need not fear I'd be mistaking the one for the other, either.'

'I just don't know,' said the lairdie.

'I might even find ways of mending the luck of those who need it,' said Lachie slyly. That brought the laird over, as Lachie knew it would.

'Well,' said the laird, 'you might have a try at it, Lachie, if you like.'

'Give me the books, then,' Lachie ordered, 'and go to bed, and leave me to get on with it.'

The laird gave the brownie his books and off he went to bed. Strangely, he slept sound that night. 'Twas the first time he'd done so since he came back to the castle.

The brownie got no sleep at all, for he sat all night over the books, and what he learned about the way the tenants paid — or didn't pay — made him pound the pages with his wee fists and grin with rage!

Folks found things weren't the same as they used to be when Lachie Tosh took over!

The letters were the start of it. They began to fall like big flakes of snow, thick and fast. Those that got them didn't fancy them much. They were all written in a very small crabbed script, and they were short and very plain-spoken. All of them told folks what they hadn't done, and to do it at once and no excuses accepted!

'Your fence wants mending. Tend to it!' said one letter.

Another one read, 'Give your shed a wash of white. Your cow is ashamed to bide in it.'

'You've twenty pounds of silver in the box hidden under your bed, that you're owing to the laird. See that he gets it,' another letter said; and still another, 'If you'd rather eat well than pay your rent go do it elsewhere.'

There were more of them, and all of them were the unpleasant sort, like the ones you've heard about. All were signed 'Lachie Tosh, Factor.'

Folks went around asking each other, 'Who *is* this Lachie Tosh?' Not a soul could answer that, but it was uncanny the way he knew all the secrets anyone had. He knew everything, and he let folks know he knew, and what he knew. The lazy ones, the thriftless ones, the dishonest ones had no peace at all! For whoever he was or wherever he came from, it was sure he had a terrible rough tongue — in his letters. But nobody ever got the bit of a sight of him.

It was no use to rush to the castle and demand that he come forth. All they saw was the housekeeper, who gave them the sort of a welcome that sent them hurrying back home, wishing they hadn't come. And it was no use taking their troubles to the laird, for although he listened politely all he said at the end was, 'You'll have to take it up with the factor.'

So they all soon learned it saved them trouble to do

what they were told and no fuss about it. As for those who were too lazy to mend their ways they were told to pack up their families and go. And they did that, and a good riddance it was.

Och aye! The good times was over, for the lairdie had got him a factor!

It was wonderful the way things got better. Farms looked like farms and as if farmers had the lease of them. The church roof got mended and so did the houses along the village street.

It was a wonder to see, too, how things picked up for those whose luck wanted mending. This one got health, that had lacked it for a year. Another one's lad heard of a place in town needing a young fellow, and went and got took on. The oldest lass of a widow had a chance to go into service where she was happy and well paid. So both of them were able to send money to help out at home. Little by little the ill luck went away, and none of the folks on the laird's estate remembered it any more.

When the next quarter day come around it was a treat to see folks coming up to the castle to pay what they owed. When it was over Lachie Tosh came out of the cupboard where he'd been hiding to keep an eye on them all and make sure all paid up as they should.

He came out, rubbing his wee hands together in glee. 'Well,' said he, 'the accounts is balanced now with plenty over to spare. So now we'd better take heed to yourself, lairdie.'

'There's nothing I need,' said the laird. ' 'Tis yourself should have something, Lachie, for all of the toil and trouble has been yours.'

'Och! You and your heart of gold!' scolded Lachie.

53

'With all of us living off you now, from me down to the least bairn of my sons' sons' sons! Let us have no more foolish talk!'

And then the brownie added, 'There's two things you need, and the first one's clothes. You're that threadbare I'm ashamed to see you walking out, lest the clothes on your back leave you entirely. So off you go to town to have the tailor make you a fine suit of clothes, and when you come back I'll tell you what is the other thing you need.'

So the lairdie went off to town, since Lachie said he had to. In a week's time he came back dressed in his fine new clothes, and there wasn't a lad to match him in looks in all of Scotland. Lachie looked him over before and behind and up and down.

'Ye'll do!' said Lachie. 'And now for the second thing you need. And that's a wife.'

'A wife!' said the laird. He sounded scared, but you could tell he was a bit pleased at the notion, too. 'But where will I be finding one?'

'Look about till you do!' Lachie told him.

'I've ne'er had o'ermuch to do with lassies. What would I be saying to her?' asked the poor lairdie.

'Och, you could ask her what she'd be thinking of brownies in the house,' said Lachie.

'Aye. I could do that,' the laird said. 'But look now, Lachie! How will I know she's the right one?'

'Do not trouble yourself about that. You'll know right enough, when the time comes,' Lachie said, 'and there'll be no way to mistake her.'

So the lairdie rode away to the North, where he had a cousin living. He met a likely lass there, and when he had a chance to get her alone he asked her, 'What do you think of brownies?'

She looked at him, surprised-like, and said in her plain North country way, 'Brownies? Och, I dinna think o' them at all! Because I dinna believe in 'em.'

Well, to be sure she wasn't the one he wanted! So he went away from there.

Then he rode to the South, and there he met as fine a lass as he had ever seen, just back from a Lady School in Edinbro'. She was not only handsome, but terribly well learned, too. So, after they got better aquainted he asked her, 'What would your opinion be of brownies in the house?'

'My good man,' said she in her fancy Lady School voice, 'the idea of the existence of brownies is the attempt of the common people to explain the disappearance of the ancient Picts!'

The lairdie got away from there in a hurry! Whew! That one would never do at all!

He had another cousin living in the East, so he rode over there. He liked the looks of a lass he found in his cousin's house, for she was a bonnie wee thing, not much bigger than a brownie herself. He soon got friendly with her, so one evening he asked her, 'What would you be thinking of a brownie in the house?'

At that she threw up her hands and screamed! 'Oh!' she cried. 'I couldn't bear the thought of it! The horrid little things! And in the house! Oh no!'

Well, the lairdie wouldn't want that one and no mistake about it!

And now there was no place to ride to, except to the West. But he fared no better there. For when he asked his question of a lass he found there, she said, 'I've never given it a thought, but I'm fair certain I'd not be liking them at all.'

So there he was, with nothing to do but ride home and tell Lachie he couldn't find the right lass, North, South, East, or West.

As he was riding home he came by the mill the brownies had flitted from. There, on a bench by the door of the mill, sat a bonnie lass with her hands in her lap. It was the miller's daughter, and she was feeling sad, for she and the wife her father had brought from town didn't get on well, having different notions about almost everything.

When the lairdie saw her, his heart gave a jump for here was a lass he could fancy! So he stopped his horse, and gave her a good day.

She looked up at him, and he looked down at her, and he asked her, 'What do you think of brownies in the house?'

She had been weeping and there were tears in her eyes, but she smiled through the tears and she said, 'Och, the dear wee things! There were always brownies at the mill when my mother was alive!'

So he took her up on his horse with him and off he rode to the castle, to tell Lachie he'd found the lass he wanted for his wife.

Lachie looked at her and he looked at the laird and he smiled all over his face.

'You went too far afield, my lad,' said he. 'I could have told you so. She's the one I was thinking of when I told you to look about!'

So the laird married the miller's daughter, and it was a grand big wedding. All the brownies, from Lachie to the least one, came to it, too, for the lairdie and the miller's daughter said there'd be no wedding at all unless the brownies were there. It was strange that none of the other guests noticed them, but it must have been because they were enjoying themselves too much to pay any heed to the wee folks!

And ever after all went well, and why should aught go wrong, with the castle full of brownies, and Lachie Tosh for the factor, and a lass who loved the brownies, and a laird with a heart of gold!

The Stolen Bairn and the Sìdh

THERE WAS a path that ran along near the edge of a
cliff above the sea, and along this path in the gloaming
of a misty day, came two fairy women of the Sìdh. All
of a sudden both of them stopped and fixed their eyes
on the path before them. There in the middle of the
path lay a bundle. Though naught could be seen of
what was in it, whatever it was moved feebly and
made sounds of an odd, mewling sort.

The two women of the Sìdh leaned over and pushed
away the wrappings of the bundle to see what they
had found. When they laid their eyes upon it, they
both stood up and looked at each other.

' 'Tis a bairn,' said the first of them.

' 'Tis a mortal bairn,' said the other.

Then they looked behind them and there was nothing there but the empty moor with the empty path
running through it. They turned about and looked
before them and saw no more than they had seen
behind them. They looked to the left and there was
the rising moor again with nothing there but the
heather and gorse running up to the rim of the sky.
And on their right was the edge of the cliff with the
sea roaring below.

Then the first woman of the Sìdh spoke and she
said, 'What no one comes to be claiming is our own.'
And the second woman picked up the bairn and hap-

ped it close under her shawl. Then the two of them made off along the path faster than they had come and were soon out of sight.

About the same time, two fishermen came sailing in from the sea with their boat skirling along easy and safe away from the rocks. One of them looked up at the face of the black steep cliff and let out a shout.

'What's amiss?' asked the other.

'I'm thinking someone's gone over the cliff!' said the first man. 'Do you not see?'

The other one peered through the gloaming. 'I see a bit of somewhat,' said he. 'Happen 'tis a bird.'

'No bird is so big,' said the first fisherman, and he laid his hand on the tiller of the boat.

'You'll not be going in! The boat'll break up on the rocks!' cried his companion.

'Och, we'll not break up. Could I go home and eat my supper in peace thinking that some poor body might be lying out here and him hurt or dying?' And he took the boat in.

It came in safe, and they drew it above the waves. Up the cliff the two of them climbed and there they found a young lass lying on a shelf of rock. They got her down and laid her in the boat, and off they sailed for home.

When they got there, they gave her over to the women to nurse and tend. They found that she was not so much hurt as dazed and daft. But after two days she found her wits and looked up at them.

'Where is my babe?' she cried then. 'Fetch my bairn to me!'

At that, the women drew back and looked at one another, not knowing what to say. For they surely had no bairn to give her!

At last one old cailleach went over to her and said, 'Poor lass. Call upon your Creator for strength! There was no bairn with you upon the cliff. Happen he fell from your arms to the sea.'

'That he did not!' she cried impatiently. 'I wrapped him warm and laid him safe on the path while I went to search for water for him to drink. I did not have him with me when I fell. I must go and find him!'

But they would not let her go, for she was still too weak from her fall o'er the cliff. They told her the men would go by the path and fetch the bairn to her. So the men went, and they walked the path from one end to the other, but never a trace of the bairn did they find. They searched the whole of the livelong day, and at night they came back and told her. They tried to comfort her as well as they could. He'd surely been found, they said, by a passer-by, and he'd be safe and sound in some good soul's house. They'd ask around. And so they did. But nobody had seen the child at all.

She bided her time till her strength came back. Then she thanked them kindly for all they'd done and said she'd be going now to find her bairn. He was all she had in the world, for his father was dead.

The fisherfolk would have had her remain with them. They'd long given the child up for dead, and they'd learned to love her well.

'I'll come back and bide with you when I have my bairn again,' said she. 'But until then, farewell.'

She wandered about from croft to croft and from village to village, but no one had seen him nor even so much as heard of anyone finding such a bairn. At last in her wandering she came to a place where some gipsies had made their camp. 'Have you seen my bairn?' she asked. For she knew they travelled far and wide and she hoped that they might know where he was. But they could tell her nothing except that all the bairns they had were their own. She was so forlorn and weary that they felt pity for her. They took her in and bathed her tired feet and fed her from their own pot.

When they had heard her story, they said she must bide with them. At the end of the week they'd be journeying north to meet others of their clan. They had an ancient grandmother there who had all the wisdom in the world. Perhaps she'd be able to help.

So she stayed with the gipsies and travelled northwards with them. When they got there, they took her to the ancient grandmother and asked her to help the lass.

'Sit thee down beside me,' the old crone said, 'and let me take thy hand.' So the grieving lass sat down beside her and there the two of them stayed, side by side and hand in hand.

The hours went by and night came on and when it was midnight the ancient grandmother took her hand from the lass's hand. She took herbs from the basket which stood at her side and threw them on the fire. The fire leapt up, and the smoke that rose from the burning herbs swirled round the old gipsy's head. She looked and listened as the fire burned hot. When it had died down, she took the lass's hand again and fondled it, weeping sorrowfully the while.

'Give up thy search, poor lass,' said she, 'for thy bairn has been stolen away by the Sìdh. They have taken him into the Sìdhean, and what they take there seldom comes out again.'

The lass had heard tell of the Sìdh. She knew that there were no other fairies so powerful as they.

'Can you not give me a spell against them,' she begged, 'to win my bairn back to me?'

The ancient grandmother shook her head sadly. 'My wisdom is only as old as man,' she said. 'But the wisdom of the Sìdh is older than the beginning of the world. No spell of mine could help you against them.'

'Ah, then,' said the lass, 'if I cannot have my bairn back again, I must just lie down and die.'

'Nay,' said the old gipsy. 'A way may yet be found. Wait yet a while. Bide here with my people till the day we part. By that time I may find a way to help you.'

When the day came for the gipsies to part and go their separate ways, the old gipsy grandmother sent for the lass again.

'The time has come for the people of the Sìdh to gather together at the Sìdhean,' said she. 'Soon they will be coming from all their corners of the land to meet together. There they will choose one among them to rule over them for the next hundred years. If you can get into the Sìdhean with them, there is a way that you may win back your bairn for yourself.'

'Tell me what I must do!' said the lass eagerly.

'For all their wisdom, the Sìdh have no art to make anything for themselves,' said the old gipsy woman. 'All that they get they must either beg or steal. They have great vanity and desire always to possess a thing which has no equal. If you can find something that has not its like in all the world you may be able to buy your bairn back with it.'

'But how can I find such a thing?' asked the lass. 'And how can I get into the Sìdhean?'

'As for the first,' the old grandmother said, 'I am not able to tell you. As for the second, perhaps you might buy your way into the Sìdhean.' Then the old gipsy woman laid her hand on the lass's head and blessed her and laid a spell upon her that she might be safe from earth and air, fire and water, as she went on her way. And having done for her all that she could, she sent her away.

The gipsies departed and scattered on their ways, but the lass stayed behind, poring over in her mind the things that she had been told.

'Twould be not one but two things she must have. One would buy her into the Sìdhean, and the other would buy her bairn out of it. And they must be rich and rare and beyond compare, with no equal in the world, or the Sìdh would set no value upon them. Where could a poor lass like herself find the likes of that?

She couldn't think at all at first because her mind was in such a maze. But after a while she set herself to remember all the things she'd ever been told of that folks spoke of with wonder. And out of them all, the rarest things that came to her mind were the white cloak of Nechtan and the golden stringed harp of Wrad. And suddenly her mind was clear and she knew what she must do.

Up she got and made her way to the sea. There she went up and down, clambering over the sharp rocks, gathering the soft white down shed from the breasts of the eider ducks that nested there.

The rocks neither cut nor bruised her hands and feet, nor did the waves beat upon her with the rising tide. The heat of the sun did her no harm, and the gales and tempests held away from her and let her work in peace. True it was, the spell of the ancient gipsy grandmother protected her from earth and water, fire and air.

When she had gathered all the down she needed, she sat herself down and wove a cloak of it so soft and white that one would have thought it a cloud she had caught from the sky.

When the cloak was finished, she cut off her long golden hair. She put a strand of it aside and with the rest she wove a border of golden flowers and fruits and leaves all round the edges of the cloak. Then she laid the cloak under a bit of gorse.

Off she went, hunting up and down the shore, seeking for something to make the frame of her harp. And she found the bones of some animal of the sea, cast up by the waves. They were bleached by the sun and smoothed by the tides till they looked like fine ivory. She bent them and bound them till she had a frame for the harp. Then she strung it with strings made from the strand of hair she had laid aside. She stretched the strings tight and set them in tune and then she played upon it. And the music of the harp was of such sweetness that the birds lay motionless on the air to listen to it.

She laid the cloak on her shoulders and took the harp on her arm and set off for the Sìdhean. She travelled by high road and byroad, by open way and by secret way, by daylight and by moonlight, until at last she came to the end of her journey.

She hid herself in a thicket at the foot of the Sìdhean. Soon she could see the Sìdh people coming. The lass watched from behind the bushes as they walked by. They were a tall dark people with little in size or feature to show that they belonged to the fairy folk, except that their ears were long and narrow and pointed at the top and their eyes and brows were set slantwise in their faces.

As the lass had hoped, one of the Sìdh came late, after all the rest had passed by into the Sìdhean. The lass spread out the cloak to show it off at its best. She stepped out from the thicket and stood in the way of the fairy. The woman of the Sìdh stepped back and looked into her face. 'You are not one of us!' she cried angrily. 'What has a mortal to do at a gathering of the Sìdh?'

And then she saw the cloak. It flowed and rippled from the collar to the hem, and the gold of the border shone as the sea waves shine with the sun upon them. The Sìdh woman fell silent, but her slanting eyes swept greedily over the cloak and grew bright at the sight of it.

'What will you take for the cloak, mortal?' she cried. 'Give it to me!'

'The cloak is not for sale,' said the lass. Cunningly she swirled its folds so the light shimmered and shone upon it, and the golden fruits and flowers glowed as if they had life of their own.

'Lay the cloak on the ground and I'll cover it over with shining gold, and you may have it all if you'll leave me the cloak,' the fairy said.

'All the gold of the Sìdh cannot buy the cloak,' said the lass. 'But it has its price . . .'

'Tell me then!' cried the Sìdh woman, dancing with impatience. 'Whate'er its price you shall have it!'

'Take me with you into the Sìdhean and you shall have the cloak,' the lass said.

'Give me the cloak!' said the fairy, stretching her hand out eagerly. 'I'll take you in.'

But the lass wouldn't give the cloak up yet. She knew the Sìdh are a thieving race that will cheat you if ever they can.

'Och, no!' she said. 'First you must take me into the Sìdhean. Then you may take the cloak and welcome.'

So the fairy caught her hand and hurried her up the path. As soon as they were well within the Sìdhean the lass gave up the cloak.

When the people of the Sìdh saw that a mortal had come among them, they rushed at her to thrust her out. But the lass stepped quickly behind the fairy who had brought her in. When the fairy people saw the cloak they forgot the lass completely. They all crowded about the one who had it, reaching to touch it and begging to be let try it on.

The lass looked about her and there on a throne at the end of the hall she saw the new king of the Sìdh. The lass walked through the Sìdh unheeded and came up to him boldly, holding the harp up for him to see.

'What have you there, mortal?' asked the king.

' 'Tis a harp,' said the lass.

'I have many a harp,' said the king, showing but little interest.

'But never a one such as this!' the lass said. And she took the harp upon her arm and plucked the golden strings with her fingers. From the harp there rose upon the air one note filled with such wild love and longing that all the Sìdh turned from the cloak to wonder at it.

The king of the Sìdh stretched out both hands. 'Give me the harp!' he cried.

'Nay!' said the lass. ' 'Tis mine!'

A crafty look came into the king's eyes. But he only

66

said idly, 'Och, well, keep it then. But let me try it once to see if the notes are true.'

'They're true enough,' the lass answered. 'I set it in tune with my own hands. It needs no trying.' She knew well that if he ever laid his hands upon it, she'd never get it back into her own.

'Och, well,' said the king. ' 'Tis only a harp after all. Still, I've taken a fancy to it. Name your price and mayhap we'll strike a bargain.'

'That I'd not say,' said the lass. 'I made the harp with my own hands and I strung it with my own golden hair. There's not another its like in the world. I'm not liking to part with it at all.'

The king could contain himself no longer. 'Ask what you will!' he cried. 'Whatever you ask I'll give. But let me have the harp!'

And now she had him!

'Then give me my bairn your women stole from the path along the black cliff by the sea,' said the lass.

The king of the Sìdh sat back on his throne. This was a price he did not want to pay. He had a mind to keep the bairn amongst them.

So he had them bring gold and pour it in a great heap at her feet.

'There is a fortune your king himself might envy,' he said. 'Take all of it and give me the harp.'

But she only said, 'Give me my bairn.'

Then he had them add jewels to the heap till she stood waist-deep in them. 'All this shall be yours,' he tempted her. ' 'Tis a royal price for the harp.'

But she stood steadfast and never looked down at the jewels.

'Give me my bairn!' said she.

When he saw that she would not be moved, he had

to tell them to fetch the child for her. They brought the bairn and he knew his mother at once and held out his arms to her. But the king held him away from her and would not let her take him.

'The harp first!' said the king.

'The bairn first!' said the lass. And she would not let him lay hand on the harp till she had what she wanted. So the king had to give in. And once she had the child safe in her arms, she gave up the harp.

The king struck a chord upon the harp and then he began to play. The music rose from the golden strings and filled all the Sìdhean with music so wonderful that all the people of the Sìdh stood spellbound in their tracks to listen. So rapt were they that when the lass walked out of the Sìdhean with her bairn in her arms, they never saw her go. So, she left them there with the king on his throne playing his harp, and all of the people of the Sìdh standing still to listen — maybe for the next hundred years for all anyone knows.

The lass took her bairn back to the fisherfolk who had been kind to her, as she'd promised to do. And she and her bairn dwelt happily there all the rest of their days.

The Woman Who Flummoxed the Fairies

THERE WAS a woman once who was a master baker. Her bannocks were like wheaten cakes, her wheaten cakes were like the finest pastries, and her pastries were like nothing but Heaven itself in the mouth!

Not having her match, or anything like it, in seven counties round she made a good penny by it, for there wasn't a wedding nor a christening for miles around in the countryside but she was called upon to make the cakes for it, and she got the trade of all the gentry as well. She was fair in her prices and she was honest, too, but she was that goodhearted into the bargain. Those who could pay well she charged aplenty, but when some poor body came and begged her to make a wee bit of a cake for a celebration and timidly offered her the little money they had for it, she'd wave it away and tell them to pay her when they got the cake. Then she'd set to and bake a cake as fine and big as any she'd make for a laird, and she'd send it to them as a gift, with the best respects of her husband and herself to the wedding pair or the parents of the baby that was to be christened, so nobody's feelings were hurt.

Not only was she a master baker, but she was the cleverest woman in the world; and it was the first that got her into trouble, but it was the second that got her out of it.

The fairies have their own good foods to eat, but

they dearly love a bit of baker's cake once in a while, and will often steal a slice of one by night from a kitchen while all the folks in a house are sleeping.

In a nearby hill there was a place where the fairies lived, and of all cakes the ones the fairies liked best were the ones this master baker made. The trouble was, the taste of one was hard to come by, for her cakes were all so good that they were always eaten up at a sitting, with hardly a crumb left over for a poor fairy to find.

So then the fairies plotted together to carry the woman away and to keep her with them always just to bake cakes for them.

Their chance came not long after, for there was to be a great wedding at the castle with hundreds of guests invited, and the woman was to make the cakes. There would have to be so many of them, with so many people coming to eat them, that the woman was to spend the whole day before the wedding in the castle kitchen doing nothing but bake one cake after another!

The fairies learned about this from one of their number who had been listening at the keyhole of the baker's door. They found out, too, what road she'd be taking coming home.

When the night came, there they were by a fairy mound where the road went by, hiding in flower cups, and under leaves, and in all manner of places.

When she came by they all flew out at her. 'The fireflies are gey thick the night,' said she. But it was not fireflies. It was fairies with the moonlight sparkling on their wings.

Then the fairies drifted fern seed into her eyes, and all of a sudden she was that sleepy that she could go not one step farther without a bit of a rest!

'Mercy me!' she said with a yawn. 'It's worn myself out I have this day!' And she sank down on what she took to be a grassy bank to doze just for a minute. But it wasn't a bank at all. It was the fairy mound, and once she lay upon it she was in the fairies' power.

She knew nothing about that nor anything else till she woke again, and found herself in fairyland. Being a clever woman she didn't have to be told where she was, and she guessed how she got there. But she didn't let on.

'Well now,' she said happily, 'and did you ever! It's all my life I've wanted to get a peep into fairyland. And here I am!'

They told her what they wanted, and she said to herself, indeed she had no notion of staying there the rest of her life! But she didn't tell the fairies that either.

'To be sure!' she said cheerfully. 'Why you poor wee things! To think of me baking cakes for everyone else, and not a one for you! So let's be at it,' said she, 'with no time wasted.'

Then from her kittiebag that hung at her side she took a clean apron and tied it round her waist, while the fairies, happy that she was so willing, licked their lips in anticipation and rubbed their hands for joy.

'Let me see now,' said she, looking about her. 'Well, 'tis plain you have nothing for me to be baking a cake with. You'll just have to be going to my own kitchen to fetch back what I'll need.'

Yes, the fairies could do that. So she sent some for eggs, and some for sugar, and some for flour, and some for butter, while others flew off to get a wheen of other things she told them she had to have. At last all was ready for the mixing and the woman asked for

71

a bowl. But the biggest one they could find for her was the size of a teacup, and a wee dainty one at that.

Well then, there was nothing for it, but they must go and fetch her big yellow crockery bowl from off the shelf over the water butt. And after that it was her wooden spoons and her egg whisk and one thing and another, till the fairies were all fagged out, what with the flying back and forth, and the carrying, and only the thought of the cake to come of it kept their spirits up at all.

At last everything she wanted was at hand. The woman began to measure and mix and whip and beat. But all of a sudden she stopped.

' 'Tis no use!' she sighed. 'I can't ever seem to mix a cake without my cat beside me, purring.'

'Fetch the cat!' said the fairy king sharply.

So they fetched the cat. The cat lay at the woman's feet and purred, and the woman stirred away at the bowl, and for a while all was well. But not for long.

The woman let go of the spoon and sighed again. 'Well now, would you think it?' said she. 'I'm that used to my dog setting the time of my beating by the way he snores at every second beat that I can't seem to get the beat right without him.'

'Fetch the dog!' cried the king.

So they fetched the dog and he curled up at her feet beside the cat. The dog snored, the cat purred, the woman beat the cake batter, and all was well again. Or so the fairies thought.

But no! The woman stopped again. 'I'm that worrited about my babe,' said she. 'Away from him all night as I've been, and him with a new tooth pushing through this very week. It seems I just can't mix . . .'

'Fetch that babe!' roared the fairy king, without waiting for her to finish what she was saying. And they fetched the babe.

So the woman began to beat the batter again. But when they brought the babe, he began to scream the minute he saw her, for he was hungry, as she knew he would be, because he never would let his dadda feed him his porridge and she had not been home to do it.

'I'm sorry to trouble you,' said the woman, raising her voice above the screaming of the babe, 'but I can't stop beating now lest the cake go wrong. Happen my husband could get the babe quiet if . . .'

The fairies didn't wait for the king to tell them what to do. Off they flew and fetched the husband back with them. He, poor man, was all in a whirl, what with things disappearing from under his eyes right and left, and then being snatched through the air himself the way he was. But here was his wife, and he knew where she was things couldn't go far wrong. But the baby went on screaming.

So the woman beat the batter, and the baby screamed, and the cat purred, and the dog snored, and the man rubbed his eyes and watched his wife to see what she was up to. The fairies settled down, though 'twas plain to see that the babe's screaming disturbed them. Still, they looked hopeful.

Then the woman reached over and took up the egg whisk and gave the wooden spoon to the babe, who at once began to bang away with it, screaming just the same. Under cover of the screaming of the babe and the banging of the spoon and the swishing of the egg whisk the woman whispered to her husband, 'Pinch the dog!'

'What?' said the man. But he did it just the same —
and kept on doing it.

'Tow! ROW! ROW!' barked the dog, and added his
voice to the babe's screams, and the banging of the
wooden spoon, and the swishing of the egg whisk.

'Tread on the tail of the cat!' whispered the woman
to her husband, and it's a wonder he could hear her.
But he did. He had got the notion now and he entered
the game for himself. He not only trod on the tail of
the cat, but he kept his foot there while the cat
howled like a dozen lost souls.

So the woman swished, and the baby screamed, and
the wooden spoon banged, and the dog yelped, and
the cat howled, and the whole of it made a terrible
din. The fairies, king and all, flew round and round
in distraction with their hands over their ears, for if
there is one thing the fairies can't bear it's a lot of
noise and there was a lot more than a lot of noise
in fairyland that day! And what's more the woman
knew what they liked and what they didn't all the
time!

So then the woman got up and poured the batter
into two pans that stood ready. She laid by the egg
whisk and took the wooden spoon away from the babe,
and picking him up she popped a lump of sugar into
his mouth. That surprised him so much that he stopped screaming. She nodded to her husband and he
stopped pinching the dog and took his foot from the
cat's tail, and in a minute's time all was quiet. The
fairies stopped flying round and round and sank
down exhausted.

And then the woman said, 'The cake's ready for the
baking. Where's the oven?'

The fairies looked at each other in dismay, and at

last the fairy queen said weakly, 'There isn't any oven.'

'What!' exclaimed the woman. 'No oven? Well then, how do you expect me to be baking the cake?'

None of the fairies could find the answer to that.

'Well then,' said the woman, 'you'll just have to be taking me and the cake home to bake it in my own oven, and bring me back later when the cake's all done.'

The fairies looked at the babe and the wooden spoon and the egg whisk and the dog and the cat and the man. And then they all shuddered like one.

'You may all go!' said the fairy king. 'But don't ask us to be taking you. We're all too tired.'

'Och, you must have your cake then,' said the woman, feeling sorry for them now she'd got what she wanted, which was to go back to her own home, 'after all the trouble you've had for it! I'll tell you what I'll do. After it's baked, I'll be leaving it for you beside the road, behind the bank where you found me. And what's more I'll put one there for you every single week's end from now on.'

The thought of having one of the woman's cakes every week revived the fairies so that they forgot they were all worn out. Or almost did.

'I'll not be outdone!' cried the fairy king. 'For what you find in that same place shall be your own!'

Then the woman picked up the pans of batter, and the man tucked the bowls and spoons and things under one arm and the baby under the other. The fairy king raised an arm and the hill split open. Out they all walked, the woman with the pans of batter, the man with the bowls and the babe, and the dog and the cat at their heels. Down the road they walked and back to their own house, and never looked behind them.

When they got back to their home the woman put the pans of batter into the oven, and then she dished out the porridge that stood keeping hot on the back of the fire and gave the babe his supper.

There wasn't a sound in that house except for the clock ticking and the kettle singing and the cat purring and the dog snoring. And all those were soft, quiet sounds.

'I'll tell you what,' said the man at last. 'It doesn't seem fair on the rest of the men that I should have the master baker and the cleverest woman in the world all in one wife.'

'Trade me off then for one of the ordinary kind,' said his wife, laughing at him.

'I'll not do it,' said he. 'I'm very well suited as I am.'

So that's the way the woman flummoxed the fairies. A good thing she made out of it, too, for when the cake was baked and cooled the woman took it up and put it behind the fairy mound, as she had promised. And when she set it down she saw there a little brown bag. She took the bag up and opened it and looked within, and it was full of bright shining yellow gold pieces.

And so it went, week after week. A cake for the fairies, a bag of gold for the woman and her husband. They never saw one of the fairies again, but the bargain was never broken and they grew rich by it. So of course they lived, as why should they not, happily ever after.

The Lass Who
Went Out at the Cry of Dawn

THERE WAS once a lass who went out at the cry of
dawn to wash her face in the morning dew to make it
bonnier, and she never came home again.

Her father searched for her, and her mother wept
for her, but all her father's searching and her mother's
greeting didn't fetch the lass back home.

She had a younger sister who loved her dearly, and
who said she'd go herself into the wide world and
travel about to find her sister and she'd not come home
till she found her, for she wasn't content to bide at
home without her.

So her father gave the younger sister his blessing
to take along with her, and a purse with a piece of
gold in it to help her on her way.

Her mother made up a packet of things for her to
take along. There was a bobbin of yarn and a golden
needle, a paper of pins and a silver thimble, and a wee
sharp knife all done up in a fair white towel. And she
had her mother's blessing, too.

She wandered up and down the world for many a
weary day. Then in her wanderings, someone told her
there was a wicked wizard who lived on Mischanter
Hill who was known to steal young maids away,
and maybe 'twas he who had taken the lass's older
sister.

Now that the lass knew where she was going, she wandered no more, but off she made for Mischanter Hill.

When she got there, she saw 'twould be a terrible hard climb, for the road was steep and rocky all the way. So she sat down on a stone at the foot to rest a bit before she went on.

While she was sitting there, along came a tinker body. He was between the shafts of a cart loaded with pots and kettles and pans, lugging it and tugging it along the stony road. He stopped when he saw the younger sister and gave her a 'good day'.

'Lawks!' said she to him. ' 'Tis a wearisome task to be doing the work of a horse.'

' 'Tis that!' the tinker agreed, 'but beggars cannot be choosers. I've no money to buy a horse so I must just go on moiling and toiling with my load.'

'Well now,' said she, 'I've a bit of gold my father gave me I've ne'er had need for. 'Tis doing nobody any good while it lies in my pocket. Take it and welcome, and buy yourself a horse.'

The tinker took the purse in his hand and looked at her. 'I've been pulling that load for a weary long time,' said he, 'and though I've met many on my way, not one has given me as much as a kind word before. If you are going up the hill to the wizard's castle, I'll give you a few words to take along with you. What you see and what you hear are not what they seem to be. And my advice to you is that you'd better far go back the way you came, for the wizard who lives at the top of the hill will enchant you if he can. But I doubt you'll heed it.'

'That I won't,' said the lass. 'But thank you kindly, anyway.' So the tinker turned his cart about and went back down the road while the lass began to climb the long steep hill.

When she got about halfway up the hill, she came across a poor ragged bodach standing by the road. His clothes were all tatters and patches, and he was pinning the rents together with thorns. As fast as he pinned them, the thorns broke, so he'd have to start all over again.

'Lawks,' said the lass. ' 'Tis wearisome work trying to mend with thorns. Now, hold a bit,' said she. 'I've a paper of pins my mother gave me that I've ne'er had use for. They're no good to anybody while they lie in my bundle. Take them and do your mending with them.'

The poor ragged bodach took the pins and he looked at her and said, 'I've stood here many a weary day, and many have passed me by, but no one ever gave me so much as a kind word before. I've naught to give in return but a few words for you to take along with you. Gold and silver are a match for evil. If you're going up to the wizard's castle, my advice to you is to turn back and go the way you came, because he's a terrible wicked wizard and he'll lay a spell upon you if he can. But I doubt you'll take it.'

'That I won't!' said she. 'But thank you kindly, anyway.'

So she left the poor bodach there, mending his clothes with the pins, and went on up to the top of the hill.

When she got to the top of the hill, there was the wizard's castle standing across a big courtyard inside a high stone wall. She opened the gates, and went across the courtyard, and knocked boldly on the castle door. The wizard himself opened it to her. The minute she saw him she knew who he was for there was such evil in his face as she'd never seen before. But he spoke to her politely enough and asked her what she'd come for.

'I'd like my older sister,' said she, 'for I hear you've brought her here.'

'Come in,' said he, throwing the door wide. 'I'll see if I can find her.' He took her into a room and left her there, and shut the door behind him.

She looked about the room, but there was no sign of her sister anywhere, so she sat down to wait. All of a sudden she heard flames crackling, and the room was filled with smoke. The flames sprang at her from the walls, and she could feel their heat. 'Lawks!' she cried. 'The castle's on fire!' And she was about to spring from her chair and run away from the room when she remembered what the tinker body had said: What you see and hear are not what they seem to be! Then said she, 'Och, no doubt 'tis only some of the wizard's magic arts.' So she paid the smoke and the flames no heed, and they went away.

She sat back in the chair and waited again for a while, and then she heard a voice calling and weeping. It was the voice of her sister that she was seeking, and she was calling her by name. The lass jumped from her chair, ready to run and find her sister. Then she remembered the tinker's words again. What you see and hear are not what they seem to be. Said she, 'Och, 'tis only the wizard's magic again, to be sure.' But the voice went on calling her, and she could scarce keep her feet from running to find where it came from. So she took the bobbin of yarn from her packet and bound her arm to the chair, passing the yarn round and round until it was all used up. Now she was safe, for no matter how she pulled, the yarn held fast. After a while the voice stopped calling, and the sound of the weeping died away and all was still. Then the lass took out the wee knife and cut herself free from the chair.

Just after that, the wizard came back and when he saw her sitting there, waiting, he looked surprised and not too pleased. But he told her to come along with him and maybe they'd find her sister. There were a lot of maidens came from here and there to the castle, he told her. She'd have to pick her sister out for herself.

They went along to another room and when she went in she stopped and stared. There was nothing at all in the room but seven white statues. Every one of them was as white as snow from head to foot, and they were as like each other as seven peas, and every one was the image of her sister.

'Pick your sister out,' said the wizard with a terribly wicked grin. 'You may take her along with you and welcome!' said he. He thought she'd never be able to do it.

The lass walked up and down before the statues. She couldn't for the life of her tell which one she ought to be choosing. So at last she stood still, with her chin in her hand, considering what to do next. Then she remembered the words the ragged bodach had given her in return for the paper of pins. Gold and silver are a match for evil! So she took the silver thimble out of her pocket and slipped it on the finger of the first statue. She'd no sooner done so than the thimble turned black as a coal. That wasn't her sister at all! So she tried it on the rest of the statues one by one, and the thimble stayed black as black could ever be, until it came to the last one in the line. She put the thimble on that one's finger, and the thimble shone out so bright it fair dazzled her eyes. 'I'll just take this one!' she told the wizard. As she spoke the statue moved, and there was her sister turned back to flesh and blood, with her own rosy cheeks and golden hair and clear blue eyes.

The younger sister took her older sister's hand and the two of them went out of the room and down the hall, and through the door of the castle.

When the wizard saw they were getting away from him, he nearly burst with the furious rage he had in him. With his magic arts he called up a great fierce wolf and sent it after them. The two sisters heard it come panting along behind them and they took to their heels. They ran like the wind itself, but the wolf came closer and closer. The older sister wept and said she could run no more. But the ragged bodach's words came into the mind of the younger sister. She cried out, 'Gold and silver are a match for evil!'

Quick as a wink she whipped the golden needle out of her packet, and turned to face the wolf. He came snapping and snarling up to her with his jaws wide open, ready to leap at her. She reached out and thrust the needle straightway betwixt his great red eyes. That was the end of the wolf, for he dinged down dead.

The wizard shrieked with rage, and came flying at them himself with his black cloak outspread, bearing him through the air like a pair of wings. All the lass had left was the wee sharp knife, and no words of the tinker body and the old bodach left to tell her what to do. But since the knife was all she had, she'd have to make do with it and hope for the best. She put her hand in the packet to pull it out, and somehow the knife got tangled up with her mother's and father's blessings. So when the wizard got close enough, and she aimed the knife at him, the blessings carried it straight to his heart and down he fell, black cloak and all!

Whilst they stood there getting their breath, they heard a great rumbling noise. They looked over at the castle, and it was rocking to and fro before their eyes. All of a sudden it turned to dust and settled down in a heap on the ground. Being made of the wizard's magic, it could no longer stand, now that the wizard was dead.

The two sisters had no need to run any more. They walked down the mountain as if they were walking on the clouds of the air, instead of the rocky steep road.

Halfway down they met up with a fine young man all dressed in the best of clothes. 'You'll not be remembering me, I doubt,' said he to the younger sister. 'I'm the ragged bodach you gave your paper of pins to. The wizard laid a spell on me that I'd be mending my clothes with thorns till the end of time. But now the spell is lifted, and I'm a free man once more.'

The younger sister would never have known him, had it not been that she saw his clothes were all stuck through with pins.

The three of them walked down the hill together, and what should they find there but a fine young man standing beside a grand shining coach. 'You'll not be remembering me,' said he. 'I'm the tinker body that you gave your purse with the gold piece in it to.' She'd ne'er have known him had he not taken the purse from his pocket and given it back. The wizard had laid a spell on him, too, but now that the wizard was dead, the spell was lifted and he was free.

The four of them got into the coach and drove back home. So the younger sister brought her older sister back with her, just as she'd said she would. The older sister married the fine young man with the pins, and the younger sister married the tinker body, and they all settled down together happily for the rest of their days.

The Ailpein Bird, the Stolen Princess, and the Brave Knight

ONCE IN the old times, the Good Times, when there were kings in Scotland, there was a wee Scottish princess who was stolen away from her father's castle. It was during a raid by a wicked king from another land she was taken, and her father never knew she was gone till the battle was over. Then someone came running to him, to tell the king she was lost, and the alarm was given. They searched the castle from end to end and all around it, too, but none of them found a trace of her.

By the time she was missed, the wicked king and his men were far away, and the princess over the saddle of one of their steeds wrapped in a soldier's cloak.

It was not to capture the princess that the raid was made, but to take her father's castle, for the wicked king wanted to kill her father and reign in his stead. Her father was a good king and ruled his people well, so his land prospered and he had plenty of gold.

The castle stood fast, and the wicked king and his men were driven away and had to go back to their own land without any of the gold. But as they went, one of the king's men caught up the princess and took her along instead.

When they got back home the little princess was brought before the wicked king, and he looked her over.

He saw that she was beautiful, and as he was angry because he'd lost the battle he made up his mind to keep her, to pay her father back for the beating he'd got.

He had her put among the women of his castle, and nobody but himself and his men-at-arms knew who she was; and they would not dare to tell, for he said he'd have their lives if they did.

So the poor little princess stayed in the wicked king's castle. She was not ill-treated, for they all liked her well enough, but she was unhappy, for her heart was sick for the sight of her own land and her own people. Her father could not come and get her, for he did not know where she was. He had them search for her for many a day, but at last he gave up hope of ever finding out what had happened to her and mourned her as dead.

When a year had gone by the wicked king sent for the princess. He had a black thought in his mind: to marry her to his son. He knew that he couldn't get the gold he wanted by capturing her father's castle, for he'd already tried that and it didn't come out the way he wanted. So the next best thing would be to marry his son to the little princess, and use her to pry some of the gold out of her father.

The princess came and stood before the king, and he told her what he had in his mind. She said nothing to him against it, for she knew she'd better not. But her heart sank at the thought of marrying the king's son. He was proud and cold, and she was sure he was cruel, too. She thought there was nothing she wouldn't give to be at home, and safe in her father's house again.

That day the women robed her in costly velvet and

put jewels on her neck and wrists and fingers, and she was sent down to have dinner at the king's table, for all the world to see. She sat at the king's right hand at dinner, with the king's son at her other side, and when they rose from the table, she was told to stay in the hall with the ladies of the king's court.

While they were gathered there together a wandering harper came into the hall to sing to them. He looked the company over as he sang, and he saw the little princess sitting there. He looked at her once, and he thought she was beautiful. He looked at her twice, and thought she was much too sad for one so young. But with the third look, he said to himself, 'I've seen that face before!' Where or when he couldn't tell, but he knew it was in some other, happier place.

He had been singing songs men like to hear, of warlike deeds and brave heroes, so now he sang a song for the ladies. It was a light, merry song, and the princess remembered that she had heard it before in her own land, and she smiled, remembering. It was only a wee ghost of a smile, but the harper saw it, and then he knew who she was!

There had been another king's castle he had sung in long ago, and she was the daughter of the king there and the merriest one of the court. When she smiled, everyone smiled with her. When she laughed, it was a treat to hear her! She was a bit of a lassie then, not grown up as she was now, for it was a long time ago. He had come back to that castle about a month back, and the servants there told him that the king would have no music in the castle, for he was mourning the princess who had disappeared during a battle about a year ago. Everybody said she was dead, poor lass, and their king's heart was broken by the loss of her.

87

The harper told himself that he'd lay his life on the odds that this was the same princess, and she wasn't dead at all! And he wondered what she was doing here, in this unlikely place. But he was too wise to say aloud what he thought. He was sure there was something wrong about it.

When they'd had enough of his singing the harper was sent to the servants' hall, and there he was given food and shown a place where he could sleep for the night. The king sent a man to tell him he was pleased with the singing, and that the harper was to stay at the castle and sing to them again.

While he was eating, the harper questioned the servants about the princess, but who she was or where she came from nobody could tell him. She had been at the castle for as long as a year, and now she was going to marry the king's son in about a month's time.

The harper wrapped himself in his cloak and lay down where they told him to. But he did not sleep, nor did he stay at the castle. Long before the wind of dawn had whistled in a new day he had taken his harp upon his arm and silently slipped away. He passed by the drowsy guards, and they saw that it was only the harper and let him go on.

The harper took the shortest road to the princess' father's castle, and he ate where he could and slept when he had to, and at last, towards the eve of the fourth day he came to its gates. The guards there were surprised to see him back, for he had not been allowed to sing the last time, but when he insisted and would not let them turn him away one of them agreed to take him into the hall. As for the rest, whether he might sing or not, that was up to the king.

The king frowned when he saw the harper, for

music reminded him of his daughter who had a way of singing all day long. Then he relented, for he thought of the people of the court and how little pleasure there was for them nowadays. So he called the harper to him and told him that he might sing, but must wait until the king himself had gone away. Then the king started towards the door of the hall, but the harper placed himself in his path and kneeling before him said, 'Your Majesty would not leave if he knew the song I sing is one written for him alone. Let your Majesty remain in the hall and hear if it be not strange and wonderful, and judge of its importance to himself.'

The king was a man of great courtesy and he was touched that the harper had sought to please him by making a song for him, for he had been told that the guards had turned him away the last time he came. He would listen to the song, he told the harper.

The harper struck a chord on his harp and then he began to sing. He sang of a castle (like this one) besieged by an enemy in the dark of a winter's night. He sang of the flashing of swords, and the clashing of spears, and of bowmen on the walls. He sang of the enemy driven away, and of the quiet after the battle.

Then soft his voice grew and gentle, as the harper sang of a fair young princess who was her father's dear joy. After the battle was over the princess was not in her bower, nor could she be found in the castle, and never was she seen again.

When the harper came to this part of the song the king sat up in his chair. He looked like a man who would have wept, had not all his tears run dry. He would have stopped the harper and he frowned and lifted his hand, but the harper said, 'The end is not

yet!' and hurried on with his song. And now he sang
of another castle, in the kingdom of the enemy king
who had led his men in the battle on that dark
winter's night. He sang of a fair young princess in
that wicked king's castle, blooming like a wild rose in
a wilderness. Captive was she and there was sorrow
in her eyes, for she was fated to marry the son of the
enemy king, who was as wicked as the king himself.

'Who is the white rose blooming in the wilderness,
captive and despairing, far from her own home?'
sang the harper.

And the princess' father gave a great cry, and
jumped from his chair. He seized the harper by the
arm and dashed his harp to the ground. His eyes
flashed and his face was terrible, and he shouted,
'Who? Who? Harper, *tell me her name!*'

The harper was not daunted by the king. He looked
the king straight in the eyes, and the name he spoke
was that of the king's lost daughter.

Then rose a shout of rejoicing from all the court
assembled that made the whole castle ring. And all the
people who were not in the hall came running, and
when they heard the news they, too, rejoiced. From
highest to lowest, there had not been such happiness upon the faces of the king's people since the
princess had been stolen away.

The king vowed that he would raise such an army
as never had been seen before, and march against the
castle of the wicked king and fetch his daughter home!

Now at the court there was a brave young knight
who had loved the princess long. And when he heard
what his king said there was a great fear in his heart
that when the wicked king saw the army approach,
he would know it was the father of the princess coming

to fetch her home, and therefore might do the little princess some harm. He told the other knights his thought, and, as many of them agreed with him, they went to the king, and after much argument persuaded him to let the young knight go first in disguise and try to bring the princess away. When she was safely away he would let the king know, and the army could march against the wicked king's castle.

There were at that time many friars going about from place to place, begging their way as they went, and they were well received in all places, being holy men. So the brave young man dressed himself in a coarse brown habit with a great cowl over his head, and taking a wallet over his shoulder and a staff in his hand he started out as one of these friars to rescue the princess.

The very day that the knight started on his journey the princess sat at dinner between the wicked king and his son. While they were eating, an Ailpein bird flew in through one of the tall windows seeking refuge from the force of the winter wind.

The people in the hall jumped up in terror, and shouted, 'An ill omen! An ill omen!' for it was thought to be a sign of ill luck when a bird flew into a castle in that way. The king told the guard to shoot the bird, but it flew straight to the princess. She caught the bird in her arms and clasped it to her breast, and then she turned and faced the soldier bravely. He had lifted his crossbow to shoot the bird, but he lowered it, for he could not kill the bird without killing the princess, too.

'Let her keep it, then,' said the king, 'since she fancies it.' For he was good-natured from the wine he had drunk, and from the thought of the gold he was going to get through the princess after he had married her to his son. ' 'Tis only a white falcon strayed from its keeper in the stress of the storm,' he added. 'Let her have it! 'Twill do for her to fondle until she has something better to fill her arms.' He looked at his son, and winked and laughed, and sipped at his wine again.

The Ailpein bird nestled in the princess' arms, and when she returned to her room to sleep she took it with her. When her serving-woman had gone, she pulled the cover from her window and set the bird upon the sill. She sat upon the wide sill beside it and stroked its head gently and said, 'There, pretty bird, go on your way, for the storm is over and I would not have you a prisoner as I am.'

And she wept and said, 'Ah me, that I had wings to fly to my father's house!'

Then the Ailpein bird spoke to her and said, 'I cannot take you to your father's house, for I must return to my own land. But I can take you from this castle, for you may come with me if you will.'

'I will gladly go wherever you take me!' said the princess.

She dropped her velvet gown upon the floor and laid the jewels they had given her upon it. She put on the dress she had worn when they carried her off, and then she was ready to go.

The Ailpein bird opened out his wings, and as he stretched them to their full span he grew before her eyes until he filled the whole space of the wide window. The princess stepped to the window ledge and seated herself upon his back, and away the white bird flew. He flew over field and forest and mountain, and soon the dark, sleeping castle was far behind them.

By dawn they had passed the borders of the wicked king's kingdom and three other kingdoms beside, and by nightfall they had left all the kingdoms of the world behind them and had come to a strange white land where all was a wilderness of ice and snow and in the midst of it an immense white castle.

'Here we will spend the night,' said the Ailpein bird.

A great snowy owl was the lord of this castle, and when the two birds met, they greeted each other fondly. The princess was given food to eat, and put to sleep in a bed of feathers, so warm that she never thought once of the coldness of that land.

The next morning she seated herself again upon the back of the Ailpein bird, and they took up their journey once more. All day they flew and at the end of the day they came to a strange land of fire. The skies were red with the flames of it and the earth rolled and heaved like the waves of a boiling sea. The bird took a sure way above the clouds of smoke and steam till he came to a huge black castle that stood upon the top of a tall black mountain.

'We will stay here for the night,' said the Ailpein bird.

A great black raven was the lord of this castle, and the two birds met like brothers long parted. The princess was fed and put to bed in a room where the wings of many birds fanned her all through the night, so that she never gave a thought to the heat from the plains below.

On the morning of the third day the princess and the Ailpein bird set out again, and towards evening they came to a tall mountain with steep shining sides of glass. It was so high that the top of it was hidden in the clouds of the heavens. But when they had passed over it, they came to a fair green land that stretched as far as the eye could see. The land was full of bird song, for many a tree grew on that plain and every tree was full of singing birds. In the midst of the plain rose a great golden castle that shone like the sun, but without the heat of it. Here the Ailpein bird set the princess down.

'This is my castle,' said the Ailpein bird, 'for I am the king of all the birds. Here you will be safe, and we will try to make you happy.'

So the princess lived in the golden castle, and was happy with the birds, except for the great longing that was still in her heart to be at home with her father and her own people.

Now, when the princess had reached the castle of the snowy owl the brave young knight who set out to rescue her had gone a third of his way. When she came to the castle of the black raven he had only a third of his journey left to go. But when she reached the golden castle, the young knight reached the castle of the wicked king at the very same moment.

The gate of the castle stood before him, so he pulled the cowl of his friar's robe over his head till it shadowed his face. There was no guard at the gate, so the knight went in and found the servants' hall, as the friars were used to do. Everything seemed to be in a grand turmoil in the castle, with people hurrying in and out. The servants were huddled together at one end of the servants' hall. The young knight went up to them and asked what all the bother was about. He looked like a friar, so they thought he was one, and told him their troubles at once. There had been a fair young princess staying in the castle and she had disappeared. It was three days ago they had missed her, and the king was in a terrible rage, for she was to have married his son, and the king's heart had been set on the marriage. When he was angry he was terrible, and nobody knew what he'd do. Where had she gone? Well, how could anyone say? The king had the guards thrown into the dungeon, for he said she must have slipped by them while they were sleeping. But the guards were honest men, and they swore that not one of them had closed an eye all night. Only the king wouldn't believe them. She was gone and that was sure, for there wasn't a hole or corner the king hadn't had them dig into, from the cellars to the garrets of the castle, and if she'd been anywhere they'd have found her.

The knight went and sat down on a bench by the fireplace, to ponder about it. What he was to do now he just did not know. If he went out after her which way should he go? If he stayed here and they couldn't find her he'd waste time he could have spent hunting for her. If they found her and brought her back he'd never be able to take her away, for the king would watch her closer than ever then.

An old woman came into the kitchen and she came over and sat down at the other end of the bench. The knight looked up at her once, but he paid no more attention to her. He was too busy thinking. But after a while he noticed the old woman was edging closer and closer to him, and soon she was right up beside him. He looked at her again and she said, 'Father, I haven't confessed my sins for a long time. Will you hear me?'

The knight didn't want to do that, for of course he wasn't really a friar and had no right to. But while he was wondering how to get out of it, the old woman

95

began to whisper to him, as if she were telling him her sins. But she wasn't! What she did say nearly made him jump out of his skin.

'I know who you are!' said she, and she laid a hand on his arm, as if to warn him to be careful. 'You are no friar, but a knight come to rescue the princess. I am the woman who attended her and I can help you.' Then the old woman told him that it was the Ailpein bird who had carried the princess away, and if he meant no evil towards the princess, she would tell him how he could go after her.

'There is no evil in my heart,' said the knight proudly, 'only a desire to serve my lady and my king.'

' 'Tis a long journey,' the old woman told him. 'There will be great danger along the way.'

'Tell me how I must go,' said the knight, disregarding her words, 'and I will start at once.'

The old woman felt in her pocket and took something out. It was three white feathers, and she put them in his hand. 'Take these,' said she. 'I found them on the floor of the room when I went to dress her in the morning, and saw she was gone. Something told me they were nothing common so I hid them away, and when I had time I took them to a wise woman I know in the village outside the castle. It was she who told me where the princess had gone and who had taken her. She told me to keep the feathers safe for you would come, and then, if you were not afraid to go after her, I was to give them to you.'

'I am not afraid!' said the knight.

'You will have to go to the end of the kingdoms of the world,' said the old woman, 'for that is what the wise woman said. And when you get there keep on going straight ahead, no matter what lies in your path.

As for the feathers you must put them safely away, for they will help you in your hour of need.'

The knight put the feathers in his wallet. Then he asked the old woman where he could find a trusty runner, to take a message to the princess' father.

'I am going away from here,' said the old woman, 'for I will stay no longer in this wicked place. I waited only to tell you what the wise woman said. But I have the keys to the dungeon, and before I go, I shall let the guards out because they told the truth. One of them will take your message for you.'

So they arranged to meet outside the castle, and when the woman came, she had one of the guards with her. The knight gave him a message, to tell the princess' father that the princess was gone from there and he could bring on his army if he liked. As for the knight, he was going to find the princess and fetch her home.

So the guard ran off with the message and the old woman went with the knight to the end of the forest and showed him the road he'd have to take. 'Where will you go?' asked the knight as they parted.

'If your king is a good king, as you say he is,' said the old woman, 'I shall go there, and wait till you bring the princess, and then I can serve her again.' And with that she turned her back and went into the forest again, while the knight started out on his way to find the princess.

He travelled out of that kingdom and into the next, and on and on through one after another. He had no trouble finding food or a place to lay his head at night, for everyone he came to thought he was a friar, so they gave what he wanted without his having to ask for it. But at last he came to the edge of the kingdoms of the world, and there before lay the great land of ice.

He stepped out onto the ice and started across it, for he had to go straight ahead as the wise woman had said. But the ice shifted under his feet and great blocks of it hurled themselves across his path, while frost clouds bit at him like forest wolves and the cold struck through to his bones. He thought he would perish there and never see the princess again. Then he thought of the feathers the old woman had given him! He took the first one out, and as soon as he held it in his hand it turned into a soft white cloak. He wrapped the cloak about him and he felt the cold no longer. The fields of ice grew still and the frost clouds drew away from him, and he came safe to the great white castle.

The snowy owl met him at the door, and the knight begged leave of him to come in and break his fast and rest before he travelled on.

'You may come in,' said the snowy owl, 'but before you eat or sleep you must strive with me to see which is the strongest.'

With that he struck his beak thrice on the floor and his feathers fell away. He stepped out of them, a tall young man with red-gold hair, in the pride of his strength.

So the two of them grappled and the struggle began. All through the night they fought and the walls of the castle rocked and groaned with the greatness of their striving. But when day broke, neither of them had bested the other.

'Hold!' said the red-haired man. ' 'Tis enough! For we are equals and neither of us has won. By that I know there is no evil in you. Now I shall take you for a brother and I will help you.'

The snowy owl took on his feathers again and had food and drink brought. While the knight was eating he told the owl his story.

'The Ailpein bird was here not long ago,' said the snowy owl. 'And there was a fair lady with him. If she is the one you seek I will help you on your journey when you have rested.'

All that day the knight slept well and warm in the cloak of feathers. At nightfall the owl woke him and told him to leave the cloak behind for he would no longer need it. He took the knight on his back and carried him to the end of the land of ice, and there he set him down.

'I can go no farther,' said the snowy owl. 'Farewell brother! You must go on alone.' And back he flew to his own white castle.

The knight looked ahead, and there before him stretched the land of fire, heaving and boiling and spurting flames and sending clouds of smoke and steam to the sky. There was no road at all to travel across it.

The knight took the second feather out of his wallet, and as soon as he held it in his hand it began to grow and turned into a great white plume that lifted him up above the fire and the smoke and the steam.

At nightfall it set him down at the door of the huge black castle on the top of the tall black mountain. At the door stood the great black raven, and when the knight begged leave to come in and break his fast and rest, the raven told him he might come in, but that he should not eat nor rest until they had striven to find out which was the stronger.

Then the raven struck his beak thrice on the floor and his feathers dropped away, and out from them stepped a tall man with black hair in the pride of his strength. The two of them grappled, and all night long they fought, while the walls of the castle shook and strained with the might of their struggle and the smoke whirled through the hall so fiercely that they could scarcely see each the other's face.

When day broke neither of them had bested the other. Then the raven cried, 'Hold! 'Tis enough! You have not won, nor have I. Now we are equals, and I shall take you for a brother and I will help you.' Then he took his feathers on again, and had food and drink brought. While the knight ate, he told the raven his story.

The raven said that the Ailpein bird had been there not long before with a fair young lady. 'If she is the one you seek,' said the raven, 'I will help you on your way when you have rested.'

The knight slept all day in the raven's castle, while the wings of many birds kept the heat of the fires below away. At nightfall the raven woke him and took him on his back to the end of the land of fire. But the great plume he left behind, for the raven told him he would need it no longer.

The raven set him down and said, 'Farewell brother! I can go no farther with you. You must go on alone.' Then the raven stretched his wings and returned to his own black castle.

The knight looked before him, and there was a great plain, and from the plain rose a mountain so high that its top was hidden in the clouds of the sky. He stepped out and travelled across the plain, and at nightfall he came to the mountain. Then he saw that the steep sides of the mountain were made of shining glass, and no man could hope to climb it.

The knight took the last feather out of his wallet, and it turned under his hand into a white wain with spiked wheels. He got into the wain and it started to climb up the mountain. All night the wain climbed, by the light of the stars and the moon. Up the mountain it went and through the clouds and down the other side. When day broke it came to the bottom and stopped. The knight stepped out of it and looked ahead of him. There before him was the wide green plain with its trees full of singing birds, and up from the trees rose the shining golden castle. And the knight knew that he had come to the end of his journey.

The Ailpein bird stood at the door of the castle when the knight came up to it. He greeted the knight courteously and asked him why he had come to the kingdom of the birds.

'I have come to take the princess back to her father,' the knight told him.

'That she must decide for herself,' said the Ailpein bird.

He sent for the little princess and she came at once. When she saw the knight her tears flowed from her eyes for joy, at seeing one who came from her own home. But she smiled through her tears for joy, too.

'This knight has come to take you home,' said the Ailpein bird. 'And though I love you well and would have you stay, I have not forgotten that you saved my life at the risk of your own, so I will not keep you if you would go.'

The princess looked long into the Ailpein bird's eyes. 'I love you well,' said she, 'even as you love me. Happy have I been here, and I do not forget that you saved me from the wicked king and his son. But I must go home.'

'Well spoken!' cried the bird. 'I would not have had you choose otherwise! A father's grief, and the love of a brave knight which has brought him through ice and fire to find you are greater claims than mine!'

They feasted that night at the golden castle, and the next day the Ailpein bird took them on his back and flew with them to the edge of the kingdoms of the world, and there he set them down.

'Farewell,' said the Ailpein bird. 'But we shall meet again!'

As they had left the white wain behind in the kingdom of the birds, the knight found horses for them in the first town they came to.

Then he and the princess rode back, into one kingdom and out of it, into another and so on and on, until they came to the wicked king's. The princess was afraid to go through the land, but she need not have had any fear, for when they got to the place where the castle had stood there was not a stone left standing of it, for the princess' father and his army had pulled it down and the wicked king and his son were dead.

When they got home at last the king was beside himself with joy at having his daughter safe home again. So what else could he do but give the brave knight his daughter's hand in marriage — if she was willing, that is, and you may be sure she was.

When they told the tale of their adventures everyone who heard marvelled. The harper made a story of it to tell at the wedding, and that's the story that you have just heard.

Everyone in the kingdom, great and small, came to see the princess married to the brave young knight.

The old woman who had given him the three feathers dressed the princess in her bridal gown, and proud she was to be the one who did it.

After they were married, while they sat at the wedding feast, three birds flew in through the window. But nobody even thought of bad luck, for they all had heard the harper's tale, so they knew who the birds were. The birds flew down and struck their beaks thrice on the floor and their feathers fell away. Then out stepped three fine young men. One had red-gold hair, and one had hair as black as the night, but the third one they had never seen before, and that one had hair as yellow as his own golden castle and he was the king of the birds.

The wedding feast lasted for a week, and then everyone went home. The three birds took on their feathers, but they did not say good-bye. 'We shall meet again!' cried they, as they flew away into the sky — and so they all did, and many and many a time.

So the king had his daughter back, and the brave knight had his princess, and she had the knight, and all of them were happy all the rest of their days.

The Changeling
and the Fond Young Mother

―――――

THERE WAS a fond young mother once who thought her babe was the bonniest in all the world. That is nothing uncommon, for every young mother thinks the same.

The trouble was that she would say it, although everyone told her not to because it was terribly unlucky.

' 'Tis what I think,' she told them. 'So why should I not say it? There never was such a bonny wee bairn as my wee bairn — so there!'

'You'll regret it,' they said. And they shook their heads and told each other, 'Just wait and see!'

He really was an uncommonly bonny lad and he thrived amazingly. That is, until the day his mother decided to step out upon the hill and pick whinberries.

She took the bairn upon one arm and the creel to hold the berries on the other, and off she went to the hill.

When she got to the place where the berries grew best, she saw a grand patch of soft green grass in an open space with the bushes all around it. So she spread her shawl there and laid the babe upon it. She knew she'd be fetching few enough berries home if she carried him along while she was doing the picking. His busy wee hands would be getting them out of the basket as fast as she put them in.

The way it is with berrypicking is that one's always seeing a better patch a little way on beyond. She kept getting farther and farther away from the place where she'd left the bairn, without taking heed of it at all. She'd gone a good piece, and had her creel well filled, when all of a sudden she heard the babe give a strange sort of cry.

'Lawks!' she cried. 'I ne'er meant to leave him so long!' And she rushed back to him as fast as legs could carry her.

The face of the bairn on the shawl was all creased and red with weeping, so she took him up to soothe him, and patted him and petted him. But he wouldn't leave off wailing, no matter what she tried. So she took him and the creel of berries, and started off for home.

He kicked and screamed all the way home, and he shook his wee fists in the air, and wailed when she laid him in his cradle. Nothing she could do would quiet him and she was fair daft with the fright it gave her.

The only time he'd stop crying was when she fed him. It seemed as though she'd never get him filled up. As soon as she gave him a spoonful of porridge, his mouth was wide open for another. He ate three great bowls of porridge, a bowl of milk and half a dozen scones, and would have eaten more had she given it to him, but she didn't have the dare. She couldn't for the life of her see where a wee thing like himself was putting it all.

From that day the babe never did thrive. He seemed to change before her eyes. His legs and arms were thin as sticks, his breastbone stuck out like that of a plucked fowl, and his head was twice too big for the rest of him. He bawled from morn till night, and all the night through, and he was always hungry no matter how much she gave him to eat. He had the face of a cross old man, all wrinkled and red it was, with the crying that never left off. His mother didn't know what to make of it at all, at all.

When folks heard about the trouble she was having with the bairn, they went to her cottage to see what they could do. But after they'd had a good look at the babe, they shook their heads and made haste to go away again.

When they were well away from the house where she'd not be hearing them, they gathered together and talked.

'We told her so!' said they.

' 'Tis plain as the nose on your face!' they said.

'We told her she'd be sorry!' said they again.

'All that foolish talk about him being so bonny. 'Twas just beggin' for trouble.' And they all nodded wisely. But not one of them would tell her what it was they were thinking. Not one.

Well, the word of the illfaring wean got to the ears of an old cailleach who lived by her lone a little bit beyond the village. She had the name for having all sorts of old wisdom, and some folks said she was a witch. When she heard the tales that were going about, she put on her shawl and shut up her house and went to have a look at the bairn.

'Tch! Tch! Tch!' she said when she got a sight of the bairn. 'Well, mistress,' said she. ' 'Tis no wonder the babe's ill-favoured. That's no bairn of your own! 'Tis a changeling that's lying there in that cradle.'

When the young mother heard that, she threw her apron over her face and burst into tears.

'I doubt ye've been goin' about telling folks how bonny your bairn was,' scolded the old woman.

'Och, I did! I did!' cried the young mother. 'Even after they told me not to.'

'Och, aye. And the fairies heard you say it. They'd not rest after that, till they got hold of your bonny bairn and put one of their ugly brats in his place. When did they change him on you?'

'It must have been whilst I was gathering whin-berries on the hill, for he's never been the same since that day. 'Twas but a wee while I was away from him, but it could have been then they did it.' And she fell to weeping almost as loud as the squalling creature in the cradle.

'Hauld your whisht!' the old woman said sharply. 'Be quiet, lass! Things are never so bad that they can't be mended, a bit at least. Run and fetch a bundle of the grass that your bairn lay on, and give me the shawl you spread for him. We'll have the fairies' babe out of the cradle and your own back in gey soon.'

The bairn's mother ran off to the hill, and found the patch of bright green grass circled round with bushes where she'd laid her babe. She gathered a great bundle of it and happed it up in her apron and fetched it back to the old woman. Then the old woman asked for the shawl the bairn had lain upon. The old woman wrapped the bundle of grass in the shawl and set it on her knee and dandled it as if it were a bairn. 'Sit ye down by the cradle,' she told the young mother, 'and neither move nor speak till I give you leave.'

Then she got a huge big cauldron and filled it full of water and set it over the fire. And all the time, she nursed the bundle of grass in the shawl. She heaped up the fire until it blazed high and the water began to steam. By and by the water began to boil in the pot and when it was boiling high and thumping away like a drum, the old woman took the bundle in one arm and a big wooden spoon in the other, and began to stir the water round and round and round. And whilst she stirred, she sang over and over in a croodling tone:

> *Fire boil the cauldron*
> *Hot, hot, hot!*
> *Dowse the changeling*
> *In the pot!*

And all of a sudden she threw shawl, grass and all, into the boiling water!

The minute she did so, the bairn in the cradle sat up with an eldritch screech, and called out at the top o' his lungs 'E-e-e-eeh! Come fetch me quick, mammy, or they'll put me in the cauldron and boil me!'

The door burst open with a terrible bang and in rushed a wild-looking fairy woman, with the young mother's bairn under her arm. She snatched the changeling out of the cradle and tossed the woman's child into it. 'Take your bairn and I'll take mine!' she screamed, and out of the door she flew.

'Well now!' said the old woman as she laid the wooden spoon on the table. 'You can take up the bairn, for it's your own. You've got him back safe again.' And she put on her own shawl and started out the door.

The bairn's mother picked up her babe and wept for joy. She ran after the old woman to thank her, but all the old cailleach said was, 'Have a care after this how you go about so braggart about your weans. 'Tis always unlucky to praise your own. A fairy might be hearing you.'

And to be sure, though that fond mother had a half

a dozen bairns more and each one bonnier than the one before, she never was known to say a word in praise of them. At least not out loud. Because you never could tell. There might be a fairy hiding somewhere near.

Michael Scott and the Demon

THERE WAS a man and his name was Michael Scott
and he was a wizard. He had the knowledge on him of
black magic and white magic and the whole of the
shades between and he was a great man entirely.

This same Michael Scott it was who stopped the
plague, when it got to Scotland, by gathering the lot
of it up into his bag and shutting it tight within. As
the plague was the De'il's own work, he put the bag
where the De'il would not be getting at it to let it
loose again. And that was in a vault at Glenluce
Abbey in Galloway where the De'il would not
be liking to go, it being too holy a place for the likes
of him.

That put the De'il against Michael Scott, so he sent
one of his demons to be troubling him at his work.

It was just the sort of a job for the demon, he being
young and full of mischief. So Michael Scott had a
terrible time of it after the demon came. What with
his pots being o'erturned, his cauldron boiling over,
his fire smoking, and one thing and another, he'd
have had less time wasted if he had just sat with his
hands folded.

It was beyond bearing! So Michael Scott set his
mind to mend matters, so that he could go on with his
magic arts in peace.

First, he tried to catch the demon, but that one was

too nimble and couldn't be caught. Then he tried to set a spell on him, but spells only seemed to make the demon livelier. So at last Michael Scott had the idea of trying to make a bargain with him.

One day, when the demon was hopping around doing whatever mischief he could, Michael Scott said to him, 'Och, now, 'tis weary work this must be for you what with all the flitting around you've got to do. Sit ye down and rest yourself for a while and let's have a gab together.'

'Och, I'm not weary at all,' the demon said. 'It suits me fine to be busy.' But being willing to oblige Michael, he perched himself on the edge of the hob, anyway.

'I can see that fine,' said Michael Scott. 'But can you not go and be busy elsewhere?'

'That I cannot,' said the demon, 'because my master has sent me to attend to you.'

' 'Tis sad,' said Michael Scott. 'Such a wearying job for a braw young lad like yourself. Is there no way you could be getting out of it?'

'There is not,' said the demon cheerfully. 'But it suits me fine, anyway.'

'Och, aye,' said Michael Scott. 'But that is for now whilst it's all new to you. However, I'm none so old and 'tis likely I'll live long. The heart of me aches to think of the long weary years you have ahead of you. It does indeed!'

The demon stopped looking so cheerful. 'That may be so,' said he, 'but nevertheless I must just make the best of it.'

'Aye,' sighed Michael Scott. 'So you must. And there's no way at all that you could be rid of the job?'

'None,' said the demon, sighing, too, in spite of himself. 'Barring one.'

'And what would that one be?' Michael asked kindly, taking care not to seem too interested and eager.

'Well, if you could be setting me a task that was too much for me so I'd not be able to do it,' the demon told him. Then he laughed and added, 'Never fear! That you ne'er could do.'

'Well, 'tis worth trying,' said Michael Scott. 'We could make sort of a game of it. 'Twould be a change for us both and make time pass quicker.'

Well, the demon could see the sense of that. He'd been overturning pots and smothering fires and the like for a fortnight past. It was a bit monotonous, if you came to look at it straight. And it could get more so as years went by. He would like a change himself for a bit of diversion.

'Give us a task then!' he said with a chuckle, being terribly sure of himself.

Michael Scott thought for a minute or two. Then he said, 'River Tweed does need a cauld to it up by Kelso Town. No man's ever been able to build one, for the water there runs too fast and deep. Would you like to be taking that in hand?'

'I will so!' said the demon, and off he went.

Michael Scott had one night to work in peace, but no more than that. The next morn, in came the demon very full of himself with his chest stuck out and a grin on his face that stretched from ear to ear.

' 'Tis done!' said he, putting a foot on the fire to set it smoking, and o'erturning a pot or two.

'Is it now?' said Michael Scott, hiding his disappointment as well as he could. 'Och! 'Tis something harder I should have asked you to do, for I'd have been able to do that myself.'

'Have another try!' said the demon, laughing at him.

'That I will,' said Michael Scott. 'You'll be knowing Ercildoune Hill where it sets in the plain like a big sugar loaf? Well then! Break it up and make three hills of it, if you can.'

'I'll be at it at once!' the demon said. 'I'll be finding it easier far than last night's work.'

So Michael Scott had another night's peace. He did no work in it but he set his wits to work for him. He sat in his chair and thought and thought and thought. He misdoubted that the demon would be back on the morrow's morn, and he wanted to be ready with a task that would free him from the demon for good and all.

Well, back the demon came the next morning, and the grin on his face was wide enough to near split his head in two. ' 'Twas no trouble at all,' he told Michael Scott gleefully. 'I'd have been back long ere this, did I not stop to hear the commotion of the people to see three hills this morn where only one was the night before. 'Tis sore befuddled and bemazed they are, to be sure!' And he screeched with laughter at the memory.

'I'm hoping you'll have something as easy and entertaining for me to do next,' he told Michael Scott.

'Och,' said Michael Scott, putting on a doleful air. 'I fear you are too much for me. 'Tis past believing the wonders you can bring about. I'm just at the point of giving it all up.'

'Och, come now,' said the demon kindly. 'Give it another try, anyway.' He looked pleased at the praise Michael had given him.

'Happen 'tis too trifling a task for a lad with powers like your own,' Michael Scott said reluctantly.

'Nay! Nay!' said the demon. 'Tell me then. I'll not be offended.'

'Well then,' said Michael hesitating-like. ' 'Tis not much, but I'd like it fine if you'd go down by the sea and make me a few fathom of rope from the sand on the shore there.'

'I will so!' cried the demon happily. 'And be back in time for my tea. 'Tis the softest task of them all!'

So off he went and left Michael Scott with a promise that he'd not be long gone.

But he never came back again. For Michael's last bidding had stumped him entirely. To this very day the demon is still there by the sea trying to make ropes of sand, and all in vain.

When the wind blows high and the waves beat the shore, if you listen you'll hear him whispering, 'R-r-r-r-ropes of s-s-s-s-sand! R-r-r-r-ropes of s-s-s-s-sand!' as he works away at the task he ne'er can do.

So Michael Scott had peace at his magic for all the rest of his days. Even the De'il himself did not bother him any more, for he was afraid if he did, Michael Scott would get the best of him, too.

The Daughter of the King Ron

MANY A strange tale is told of the isles of the Gaelic seas, but surely none so strange as that of the daughter of the great King Ron.

How many of the isles there are would be hard to say, for the counting of them would be an endless task. Some of them are great islands, with harbours and towns and people upon them, but many of them have little soil and mostly rock, and on some of these no man ever sets his foot, for where would be the use of it?

Upon these small, deserted isles the Ron delights to dwell, for the rocks are grand places for him to be sunning himself, and in the pools and the little bays around them are the fish he likes best to eat. There, too, the rocks slant down into the water, and there the young seals sport and play, slipping down the smooth grey rocks and into the cool green water with never a splash.

Now some of the seals are not like other seals, for they can change their shapes if they will, and become men and women for as long as it pleases them. Fishermen tell tales of going out into the misty dawn and seeing the likes of a great man, strong and powerful, walking upon the rocks, or of coming in with their catch after sundown with night drawing in and hearing the voice of a woman singing a strange, wild, sweet song across the waters.

But never could a fisherman come close enough to get what would be a good look at whoever was there, for the hurling waves and the cruel rocks in the water about the islands made a wall to guard them, and where the gate of it would be nobody could know.

It is from these strange ones that the seals choose their kings. Now there was once a great King Ron who had many sons but only one daughter and she the least one of the family, and at the time the tale begins she was of little age, for her childhood had not long been left behind her.

The name of the king was Ailean Mor, which means Great Rock, and a great rock he was, to be sure, both in size and in strength. His daughter's name was Fionna, the Fair One, but her father had another name for her, for he called her Fearcharagh, the Best-Beloved. She was the apple of his eye and he kept her under that eye as best he could. But to be the King Ron has not the makings of an easy life, because the clans of the seals are many and spread over many seas, and each with its own chief, ruling in his own way. Often enough the Ron Mor had to be off and away, here and there, settling differences about fishing rights and such-like arguments. As he could not take his daughter with him, she just stayed at home.

Now across the sea to the east of the isles where the seals had their homes was one less ill-favoured by nature. It was, perhaps, half a day's journey away by sail with a fair wind blowing. One of the larger of the man-isles, it had upon it not only two towns and a handful of scattered farms, but a castle, and in that castle lived the young Lord of the Isles.

He, like the Ron King, was big and powerful in

build, and handsome as a picture. He had the look to him of a man who would brook no interference with his ideas or plans. Every lass who ever knew him would shiver with delight at the proud way of him, and sigh at the beauty of him, but he put his mind upon none of them, for in all his young years he had never yet seen the maid he felt he'd like to wed. So he held his head high and passed the lot of them by without more than half-seeing them. Still, it troubled him a bit, for he knew he'd reached the age when he should marry for the sake of the family.

He'd almost made up his mind to drop all the names of the lasses he least minded marrying into a creel and pick one out, and then get on with the wedding willy-nilly.

With that on his mind he went down to the quay, and got into his boat and set out for a sail. What with thinking over all the lasses he knew, and separating the possibles from the impossibles, maybe he wasn't paying too much attention to the way he was going. At any rate, what brought him up short was a voice calling almost in his ear, and sitting up there on the rock above him, and looking down at him, was a bit of a lassie.

'Man!' said she, 'if you do not turn your boat she will break on the rocks.'

The heart of the young Lord of the Isles turned three times upside-down in his breast, while he was turning his boat once away from the rocks. The boat he turned, but his head he didn't turn the same way, for he never took his eyes from her face.

'Bide there till I come!' he called to her, and then he put his eyes to the sea to find a place where he could come in to the isle. Three times around it he sailed, and the third time he saw a narrow stretch of clear water where he might hope no sharp rocks lay in wait for the boat below the water, and win or lose in he went and brought the boat up safe on a narrow spit of sand. He leapt from his boat, and up the rocks he climbed, and there at the top was the lass.

'Who are you?' he demanded. 'And how did you come here?'

'I am the daughter of the King Ron,' said she, 'and I live here.'

He didn't know did he believe her or did he not! It might be true or she might be daft, but what he said next he had to say.

'Will you marry me?' said he.

'That I cannot say,' said she, 'till my father comes back and tells me.'

'And when will he come back then?' asked the young Lord of the Isles.

'Who can say?' she answered. 'Perhaps tomorrow. Perhaps even today. But I think it will more likely be a week away.'

'I'll be back in a week at this same hour and ask him myself,' said he. And he turned and went back down to his boat, and sailed home to his own isle and to his great grey castle.

A week to the hour and he was back again, and she was there on the rock waiting for him.

'Has your father returned?' he asked her.

'Not yet,' said she, but her eyes were on the sea. She lifted her arm and pointed. 'He is coming now,' she said.

All he saw was a silver streak far out on the western sea. Nearer and nearer it came, and then the young lord saw for a minute the shining shape of a great sleek seal. It flashed close by, and disappeared behind the rocky cliff of the isle.

Then up from the rocks came the King of the Ron, by inches broader and by inches taller than the young lord himself. A giant of a man was the King Ron, with a frown like a thundercloud on his brow and a flash of anger like lightning in his eyes and thunder itself from his mouth.

'And who are you, who dares to trespass upon the lands of the Ron!' he roared. A fearsome sight he was to see, in his wrath.

But the young lord came from a race that bred no cowards. He stood his ground and he faced the Ron and he answered firm and clear. 'The Lord of the Isles am I!' said he, 'and I have come to ask your leave to wed your daughter.'

The Ron was struck to silence, and for a while he stood frowning at the Lord of the Isles. Then the thunder cleared from his brow and the lightning from his eyes, and he turned to his daughter. 'Fearcharagh, Fearcharagh,' he said tenderly, 'what have you to say to that?'

The lass said nothing at all, but her eyes begged for what she would not put into words.

The Ron sighed a great deep sigh, and then he said sadly, 'What there is to be said has already been said, for I see you are both of the same mind.'

The three stood facing each other, and there was no sound at all but the wind blowing in the dry grass and the waves clawing at the rocks and the gulls shrieking high overhead.

Then the Ron Mor said at last, 'Come back in a month, Man, if you are of the same mind then. And if you come back bring with you such garments as the women among you wear, for my daughter may take nothing with her when she leaves the Kingdom of the Ron.'

'With nothing I will take her,' said the young Lord of the Isles proudly. 'She needs no other dower than herself when she becomes my bride!'

Then the young lord took her by the hand and looked deep into her eyes. 'I will return,' said he.

When the month had passed the Lord of the Isles came back as he had promised. He brought with him undergarments of fine linen and lace, as soft and white as the froth that tipped the sea waves. He brought a gown of rarest silk woven to his own order, that shimmered with green and blue and gold, like the sea with the sun upon it. He brought a golden coronet, jewelled with sea pearls, to set upon Fionna's soft golden brown hair, which she wore cut short upon her neck in the fashion of the seal-women.

When she had dressed herself in the garments she was the loveliest thing to see that had ever met the Lord of the Isles' eyes. Only she went barefooted, for the young lord had forgotten to bring her any shoes to wear.

When she was ready the Ron said heavily, 'Guard her well, Man, for you have taken the brightest jewel in the crown of the King of the Ron.' Then he took the young lord's hand in his left hand and his daughter's hand in his right. To his daughter he spoke and he said to her, 'This you must promise! If ever an unkind word should pass the lips of your husband when he speaks to you, you must return to the Kingdom of the Ron!'

'I do so promise!' said she.

'This must you, too, promise! If ever an unkind

word should pass your lips and you should speak to
her in anger she must leave you without hindrance and
return to the Kingdom of the Ron.'

The Lord of the Isles laughed loud and the Lord
of the Isles laughed long, in scorn at the thought of
unkindness between himself and Fionna.

'I do so promise!' he said readily.

'And this, too,' said the Ron. 'With nothing she
goes from me. Returning, she must bring nothing
with her.'

'Yes!' said they.

Then the King of the Ron joined their hands together, and he turned and went down over the rocks
away from them.

They went down to the young lord's boat and got
in, and sailed away to the island where his castle was.
But the Ron did not see them leave, for there was no
more to be seen of him by then but a silver streak on
the far-off sea, going always to the northward.

The young lord and his bride came into his island,
and there at the quay was a great shining coach with
four white horses waiting to carry them up to the
castle. All the people of town and countryside were
lined along the way to welcome them home. And
because she was very young and very beautiful they
loved her at sight. They wondered where the young
lord had found her, but when they saw her feet without shoes they thought she was a country lass that the
Lord of the Isles had found in his travels on the mainland. So they called her 'the barefoot bride,' but they
thought no less of her because of that. When they got
to know her better their love knew no bounds, for she
was ever kind and gentle in all her ways with them.

So a year and a year and two more years went by,

and the young lord and his wife were happy in their castle by the sea. At the end of the third year a baby lay in the cradle, and the young lord had his son and heir. It seemed then that no cloud could ever dim their happiness.

But a young wife is tied by the heartstrings to her child and cannot always rise and leave at her lord's bidding. It often happened that the Lord of the Isles would wish to go here and there, but the young wife would say that she must stay at home.

Proud as he was of his son this did not always suit the young lord's fancy, for in the first years where he wished to go, there she went too, and many a high junketing time they had together where all was new and wonderful to her and he the lad to show it all to her.

Now, too often, when he asked her to come with him, she would shake her head and say that the child needed her. 'Have patience,' she would say with a smile. 'Soon he will be older and I will come with you then.'

Then the Lord of the Isles would go off alone, and that did not please him at all. But although he did not complain to Fionna, patience was what he did not have at all, so it happened that soon he was away from the castle more than he was in it.

It was one of these times that the Lord of the Isles came back, and found his wife sitting at the window looking out over the sea. He had left her overlong, this time, for he had gone so far as the mainland with a party of friends and they had been delayed there over the night. He thought she looked lonely, and his conscience hurt him that he had left her so long, and he was angry with himself for his carelessness towards her. He was much too proud to say so and he shut it in.

The baby lying in his cradle was roaring away in grand style, and his mother paying no attention to it, knowing, as mothers do, that there are times when nothing ails them at all, but babies must cry in order to grow.

But the racket gave the Lord of the Isles a handle for his wrath, to turn it against somebody else, since pride would not let him turn it to himself. 'In the name of heaven, Fionna,' he cried angrily, 'is there not some way you can keep the wee lad quiet?'

She turned herself upon the window seat and slowly she rose to her feet, with her great dark eyes fixed sadly upon his face.

'Oh, my lord, my lord,' she said reproachfully. She went to the cradle where the babe now lay quiet, having finished his crying for the time. She picked up the child and kissed him, once on each cheek and once on his brow and once on his small rosy mouth, and laid him back gently in his cradle again. Then she went out of the room.

The Lord of the Isles sat down in the window seat, and waited for his love to come back again. He waited long, and the baby slept, but still she did not return. So he went in search of her, through every room in the castle. From room to room he hunted, but she was in none of them. The cook and the scullery maids had seen no hair of her, and the gardener had not seen her since the morn. Her horse stood idle in its stall in the stables, and the grooms had not seen her all the day.

So he sat down on a stone bench by the gate lodge to wait again, thinking she'd gone to the village and thinking, too, that it was strange she had not told him she was going, as she always had before.

And then he remembered the promise they had made to the Ron!

Down to the sea he tore, with his heart racing faster than his feet. But he was too late.

There on the rocks lay her clothes, piled in a tidy heap, and far out on the sea a silver streak moved swiftly away from him.

And so Fionna Nic Mor Ailean returned to the Kingdom of the Ron, according to the promise she had made to her father. For the Lord of the Isles had spoken to her in anger, and there was nothing else that she could do. And as she had brought nothing with her, so too, by the terms of her promise, she took nothing back with her. For she left her babe in his cradle, her lord in his castle, and her clothes on the rocky shore.

The Lord of the Isles went back into his castle, and shut himself up in his room. For a long week he had no word with anyone, and if he ate a bite or drank a sup no one knew of it. But when, on the seventh day, he came out, it was as if he were a different man. He, who had been wayward and proud, was gentle and humble. He, who had ruled with arrogance, was just and kind. No one in all the years to come ever heard an unkind word from him. And never did he allow Fionna's name to be mentioned to him, though all who knew her grieved that she was gone and would have sorrowed with him had he allowed it.

So it went until his child and Fionna's had grown to be a man. On the day the lad reached his twenty-first year there was a great celebration because of it, and people came from the mainland and from all the towns of the islands. Before the banquet was over, while all were gathered together, the lord handed the keys to the castle and a deed to all he possessed to his son. The lad would have refused the gift, but his father pressed it on him, so the son laid the papers and keys aside and thought to take the matter up with his father upon the next day.

But while all were feasting, the Lord of the Isles rose from the table and went down to the quay, and getting into his boat set sail to the westward. And he never came back again.

Where did he go? Well, there were many stories about that. Some said that he sailed far out on the great western ocean and was lost there in the high green waves. Some said that he sailed until he reached Tir-nan-Og, the Isles of the Blest, to live forever there in happiness with the saints he had grown to resemble.

But the fishermen, who tell the tale, say that he simply sailed to the island of the King of the Ron, taking nothing with him but himself, for his boat with all his clothes in it was found days later halfway between the quay of his own island and the mainland, right side up and with no harm done to it.

And the fishermen say that he stayed at the castle to do his duty by his son until he became a man and could go on by himself, for his father could not take him with him, any more than Fionna could when she returned to her father.

And they say that the King of the Ron took him in, for the sake of the love he and Fionna still had for each other, and gave him the power of the Ron Mor to change himself from man to seal at will.

In proof of this the fishermen say that where they once saw one great man in the mists of the dawning day on the rocks of the seals, they now see two, and with them often, a woman who sits and sings more wildly and sweetly than ever before.

So the end of the tale is a happy one, with Fionna and the Lord of the Isles together in the Kingdom of the Ron, after all the long unhappy years.

Their son lived on in the great grey castle, and became the new Lord of the Isles in his father's stead. A good one he was, too, for he followed the rule of his father, whose motto was 'be kind'.

The Bride Who Out-Talked the
Water Kelpie

A SOLDIER there was once, and he was coming home
from the foreign wars with his heart light and free,
and his bagpipes under his arm. He was marching
along at a good pace, for he had a far way to go, and a
longing in his heart to get back to his home again. But as
the sun lowered to its setting, he could plainly see that
he'd not get there by that day's end so he began to be
thinking about a place where he could bide for the night.

The road had come to the top of a hill and he looked
down to see what lay at the foot of it. Down at the
bottom was a village, and there was a drift of smoke
rising from the chimneys where folks were getting
their suppers, and lights were beginning to twinkle on
here and there in the windows.

'There'll be an inn down there, to be sure,' said the
soldier, 'and they'll have a bite of supper for me and a
place for me to sleep.'

So down the hill he went at a fast trot with his kilt
swinging, and the ribbons on his bagpipes fluttering
in the wind of his going.

But when he got near the foot of the hill, he stopped
short. There by the road was a cottage and by the door
of the cottage was a bench and upon the bench sat a
bonny lass with black hair and blue eyes, taking the air
in the cool of the evening.

He looked at her and she looked at him, but neither of them said a word, one to the other. Then the soldier went on his way again, but he was thinking he'd ne'er seen a lass he fancied so much.

At the inn they told him that they could find him a place to sleep and he could have his supper too, if he'd not be minding the wait till they got it ready for him. That wouldn't trouble him at all, said he. So he went into the room and laid off his bagpipes and sat down to rest his legs from his day's journey.

While the innkeeper was laying the table, the soldier and he began talking about one thing or another. At last the soldier asked, 'Who is the bonny lass with the hair like the wing of a blackbird and eyes like flax flowers who bides in the house at the foot of the hill?'

'Och, aye,' said the innkeeper. 'That would be the weaver's lass.'

'I saw her as I passed by on the road,' said the soldier, 'and I ne'er saw a lass that suited me so fine.'

The innkeeper gave the soldier a queer sort of look, but said naught.

'I'm minded to talk to her father,' the soldier said, 'and if she could fancy me as I do her, happen we could fix it up to wed.'

'Happen you'd better not,' said the innkeeper.

'Why not, then?' asked the soldier. 'Is she promised to someone already?' ,

'Nay, 'tis not that,' the innkeeper replied quickly. 'Only . . . Och, well! You see she's not a lass to be talking o'ermuch.'

' 'Tis not a bad thing for a lass to be quiet,' the soldier said. 'I ne'er could abide a woman with a clackiting tongue.'

128

The innkeeper said no more, so that was the end o' that.

When he'd had his supper, the soldier went out of the house and back up the road till he came to the cottage again. The bonny lass was still sitting on the bench by the door.

'I'll be having a word with your father, my lass,' said the soldier. She rose from the bench and opened the door and stood aside to let him go in. When he had gone in, she shut the door and left him standing in the room on one side of the door and herself outside on the other. But not a word did she say the while.

The soldier looked about the room, and saw at the far side a man who was taking a web of cloth from the loom.

'Is it yourself that's the weaver?' asked the soldier.

'Who else would I be?' asked the man, starting to fold the cloth.

'Then I've come to ask about your daughter.'

The man laid the cloth by, and came over to the soldier. 'What would you be asking then?' he asked.

' 'Tis this,' the soldier said, coming to the point at once. 'I like the looks of your lass and if you've naught to say against it, I'd like to wed with her.'

The weaver looked at the soldier, but said nothing at all.

'You need not fear I could not fend for her,' the soldier said. 'She'd want for naught. I have a good wee croft waiting for me at home and a flock of sheep and some bits of gear of my own. None so great, of course, but it would do fine for the lass and me, if she'd have me.'

'Sit ye down,' said the weaver.

So the two of them sat down at either side of the fire.

'I doubt ye'll be at the inn?' the weaver asked.

'Where else would one from a far place stay?' asked the soldier.

'Och, aye. Well, happen the folks at the inn were telling you about my lass?'

'What could they say that I could not see for myself?' the soldier said. 'Except that she doesn't talk o'ermuch. They told me that.'

'O'ermuch!' exclaimd the weaver. 'She doesn't talk at all!'

'Not at all?' the soldier asked.

'Och, I'll tell you about it,' said the weaver. 'She went out to walk in the gloaming a year or two ago, and since she came home that night, not a word has come from her lips. Nobody can say why, but folks all say she's bewitched.'

'Talk or no,' said the soldier, 'I'll have her if she'll take me.' So they asked and she took him.

Then they were married, and the soldier took the lass away with him to his own croft.

They settled in, she to keep the house and look after the hens and do the cooking and baking and spinning, and he to tend his sheep and keep the place outside up good and proper.

The lass and he were well pleased with each other and all went well for a while. Though she did not talk, she was good at listening and it took a time for the soldier to tell her all about himself. Then she had a light hand with the baking and a quick hand at the spinning, and she kept the house tidy and shining clean. And she had a ready smile that was sweet as a song. The soldier was off and away most of the day, tending his sheep or mending his walls or working about the croft. When he came home to the lass, the smile and the kiss he got from her were as good as words.

But when the year turned towards its end, and the days grew short and the nights long and dark, the sheep were penned in the fold and the soldier was penned in the house because of the winter weather outside. Then 'twas another story. The house was that quiet you'd be thinking you were alone in it. The soldier stopped talking, for the sound of his own voice going on and on all by itself fair gave him the creeps.

She was still his own dear lass and he loved her dearly, but there were times he felt he had to get out of the house and away from all that silence.

So he took to going out at night just to hear the wind blowing and the dead leaves rustling and a branch cracking in the frost or maybe a tyke barking at some croft over the hill. It was noisy outside compared to the way it was in the house.

One night he said to the lass, 'The moonlight's bright this night. I'll be going down the road to walk.' So after he'd had his tea, he went out of the house and started down the road. He paid little heed to where he was going, and that's how it happened he nearly walked into the horse. The horse stopped with a jingle of harness and then the soldier saw that the horse was hitched to a cart, and the cart was filled with household gear — furniture and the like. There were two people on the seat of the cart, a man and a woman. The man called out to him, 'Are we on the road to Auchinloch?'

'Och, no!' the soldier said. 'You're well off your way. If you keep on this way you'll land in Crieff —

some forty miles on. And not much else but hills between here and there.'

'Och, me!' said the woman. 'We'll have to go back.'

'Poor lass,' the man said tenderly, 'and you so weary already.'

'I'm no wearier than yourself,' the woman replied. ' 'Twas you I was thinking of.'

Suddenly the soldier said, 'You're far out of your way and you'll never get there this night. Why do you not bide the night with us and start out fresh in the morn? Your horse will have a rest and so will you, and you'll travel faster by light of day, and you'll not be so much out in the end.'

But it was not so much for them, he asked it, as for himself, just to be hearing other voices than his own in the house.

They saw he really meant it, so they were soon persuaded. It wasn't long till he had them in his house, and their horse with a feed of oats in his barn. They were friendly, likeable folks, and it was easy to get them talking, which was just what the soldier wanted. They were flitting because their old uncle had left them his croft, and they wouldn't have come at such an unseasonable time, if they hadn't wanted to settle in before the lambing began. Besides, they'd never had a place of their own, and they couldn't wait to get there. So they talked and the soldier talked, and the lass sat and smiled. But if they noticed she had naught to say, neither of them mentioned it.

The next morning they got ready to leave, and the soldier came out to the gate to tell them how to go. After he'd told them, the woman leaned over and said, 'What's amiss with your wife? Does she not talk at all?'

'Nay,' said the soldier. 'She's spoken not a single word for two years past.'

'Och, me!' the woman said. 'She's not deaf, is she?'

'That she's not!' the soldier told her. 'She hears all one says. The folks where she comes from say that she's bewitched.'

'I thought it might be that,' the woman said. 'Well, I'll tell you what to do. Back where we dwelt there's a woman that has the second sight and she's wonderful for curing folks of things. She cured my own sister after the doctors gave her up. It was ten years ago and my sister's living yet. You take your wife over there and see what she can do.' She told the soldier where to find the old body, and as they drove away, she said, 'You needn't be afraid of her for she's as good as gold. She'll never take anything for helping anybody, and if she's a witch, nobody ever laid it against her. She's just a good old body that has the second sight.'

The soldier went into the house and told his lass to get herself ready, for they were going visiting. He did not tell her why, in case it all came to naught, for he couldn't bear to have her disappointed if the old body couldn't help her at all.

He hitched his own wee horse to his cart, and he and the lass drove off to the place where the folks that were going to Auchinloch had dwelt.

They found the old body without any trouble right where the woman said she'd be. She was little and round and rosy and as merry and kind as she could be. The only thing strange about her was her eyes, for they were the sort that made you feel that nothing in the world could ever be unseen if she took the trouble to look at it, no matter where it was hidden.

When she heard the soldier's story, she said at once

that she'd be glad to help them if she could. Folks were probably right when they said the lass was be-witched, but what she'd have to find out was how it had happened. That might take time because the lass couldn't help her, since she couldn't talk.

Then the old woman told the soldier to take himself off for a walk and leave the lass with her and not to come back too soon for if he did, she'd just send him away again.

The soldier walked round and round, and at last he found the village that belonged to the place. There was a blacksmith's shop and an old stone church and a post office and a pastry shop and a little shop with jars of sweeties in the windows, that sold everything the other shops didn't have. When he'd seen them all, he went and sat in the only other place there was, which was the tavern, and the time went very slow. But at last he thought it must be late enough for him to go back and fetch his lass. Maybe he'd been foolish to bring her to the old body after all. He'd not go back if the old woman sent him away again. He'd just pack up his lass in the cart and take her home and keep her the way she was. If he'd known what was going to happen, maybe that's what he'd have done.

They were waiting for him when he got back to the little old woman's cottage, and the old body told him at once she'd found where the trouble lay.

' 'Tis plain enough,' said she. 'Your wife has offended the water kelpie. When she went to walk in the gloam-ing, she drank from the well where the water kelpie bides. And as she leaned over to drink, one of the combs from her hair dropped into the water and she never missed it. The comb fouled the water, and the kelpie can bide in the well no more till she take it out again. So angry he was, that while she drank of it, he laid a spell on the water that took her speech away.'

'But what shall we do now?' asked the soldier.

'All you need to do,' said the old woman, 'is take your lass back to the well and let her take the comb from the water.'

'And she'll talk then?' the soldier asked.

'Och, aye! She'll talk. But watch out for the water kelpie, lest he do her more harm, for he's a queer creature always full of wicked mischief and nobody knows what he may do.'

The lass and the soldier were so full of joy that they hardly knew how to contain it. The soldier wanted to pay the old woman for what she'd done, but she said it was nothing at all, and in any case she never took payment for doing a kindly service. So the soldier thanked her kindly, and he and his lass went home.

When they had found somebody to look after the croft, they started off to take the spell from the lass's tongue. When they got to the place, the soldier and the lass went out to find the well in the woods. The lass bared her arm and reached down into the water and felt around till she found the comb. She put it back in her hair, and as soon as she did, she found she could talk again.

The first thing she said was, 'Och, my love, I can talk to you now!' And the second thing she said was, 'Och, I have so much to say!'

They went back to the weaver's house, and when he found that his daughter could talk, he was that pleased. He ran about the village telling everybody, 'My lass has found her tongue again!' 'Twas a rare grand day for the weaver. And of course for the soldier, too.

The weaver and the soldier couldn't hear enough of

her chatter. They took to following her about just to listen to her as if it were music they were hearing.

After a day or two, she began to grow restless, for she wanted to go home to their own wee croft. So off they set, and she chattered to him every mile of the way. The sound of her voice was the sweetest sound he'd ever heard.

So they came home. It was still winter, and the sheep were still penned in the fold and the soldier in the house, but there wasn't a bit of silence in the cottage. There was this and that she had to tell him, and something else she must say. The soldier could hardly slip a word in edgewise, but he still thought it was wonderful to hear her.

After a month or two had gone by and the winter was wearing off towards spring, he began to notice something he had not noticed before. And that was that his bonny wee wife talked away from morn to night, and he wasn't too sure that she did not talk in her sleep. He found he had in his house what he'd told the innkeeper he never could abide — a lass with a clackiting tongue.

He would not have had her silent again; ne'er the less, a little quiet now and then would not have come amiss. But he still loved her dearly, and she was his own dear lass.

So one fine morn after the lambing was over and the sheep were out on the hillside with their dams, he went off to see the old woman who had the second sight to find out if she could do aught about it.

'Deary me!' said she. 'I misdoubted the kelpie would find a way to turn things against you.'

'That he did!' said the soldier. 'Or I'd not be here.'

'Did she drink of the water again?' the old body asked.

'She did not,' said the soldier. 'Not even a drop.'

' 'Twas not that way he got at her then,' said the old woman. 'Well, tell me what she did do then?'

'She took the comb from the water and she stuck it in her hair,' the soldier told her, 'and that's all she did do.'

'Did she wipe it off first?' the old body asked anxiously.

'Nay. She did not,' said the soldier.

'I see it plain,' the old body said. 'The water that was on the comb was bewitched again. Och, there's not a fairy in the land so full of malice as the water kelpie.'

So the old woman sat and thought and thought, and the soldier waited and waited. At last the old woman said, 'A little is good, but too much is more than enough. We'll give the kelpie a taste of his own medicine. Take your lass back to the well. Set her beside it and bid her to talk down the well to the kelpie the livelong day. The kelpie must answer whoever speaks to him, so the one of them that tires first will be the loser.'

' 'Twill not be my lass,' said the soldier. 'I'll back her to win the day.'

So he took his wife back to the well and sat her down beside it, and bade her call the kelpie and talk to him until he came back for her.

So she leaned over the well as he told her to and called to the kelpie. 'Kelpie! Kelpie! I'm here!' cried she.

'I'm here!' answered the kelpie from the bottom of the well.

137

'We'll talk the whole of the day,' the lass said happily into the well.

'The whole of the day,' the kelpie agreed.

'I've such a lot to tell you,' the lass went on.

'A lot to tell you,' the kelpie said in return.

The soldier went away, leaving the lass by the well talking so fast that her words tripped over themselves, with the kelpie answering her back all the time.

He came back when the sun had set and the gloaming lay over the wood, to find the lass still sitting there, bending over the well. She was still talking, but very slow, and he could hardly hear the kelpie answer at all.

Well, now that the day was safely over, the soldier laid his hand on her shoulder. 'Come away, lass,' said he. She looked at him so weary-like that his heart turned over with pity. He'd just take her the way she was from now on, silent or clackiting, he told himself.

She looked up and smiled at him, and then she called down the well. 'I bid you good day, kelpie. 'Tis time for me to go home.'

There wasn't a sound from the well for a moment. Then in a great loud angry voice the kelpie shouted, 'GO HOME!'

So the soldier gave his arm to the lass, and they started to walk back through the woods to her father's house. She said only two things on the way home.

The first thing she said was, 'I'm awful thirsty,' but she drank no water from the well. The soldier made sure of that!

And the second thing she said was, 'I'm tired of talking.'

Well, from that time on, she neither talked too little or too much but just enough. The soldier was content, for she was his own dear lass, and he loved her dearly.

Since the old body with the second sight would never let them pay her for the good she'd done them, they invited her to be godmother when their first bairn was born. That pleased her more than if they'd given her a sack of gold. But never again in all her days did the wife go out alone in the gloaming or drink from a fairy well.

The Drowned Bells of the Abbey

IN THE far-off days when the Picts and the Scots were dividing the ancient land of Scotland and fighting amongst themselves to decide who could get hold of the most of it, there came good men from over the seas to settle in the land.

They found places for themselves here and there along the coasts by the sea, and lived wherever they could find shelter, and fed themselves on whatever the earth and the sea were willing to give them. 'Twas a hard life, but they made no complaint, for all they did was done for the glory of God.

These men called themselves monks, and what they had come for was to spread the word of God among these strange wild people, who had never heard tell of it before. The monks were learned men and wise in the arts of knowledge and healing. They taught the people and helped them in illness and in trouble. Soon they were greatly loved because of the goodness there was in them.

There was a band of these good monks who settled in a wild deserted place at the head of a deep glen near the sea in the north of Scotland. At first there was only a half dozen of them with a leader they called their abbot. The monks made their homes in the caves along the sides of the glen.

The people of the land at the time were wild and

savage and given to the worship of demons, but the monks brought them to gentler ways and taught them to live as people lived in the lands from which they had come.

As time went by, more monks came to join the band, and the people for love of them built them an abbey so that they no longer needed to dwell in caves.

For love, too, in time the people had a peal of bells made for the chapel of the abbey. There were five bells, from the smallest silver-tongued one to the great bell which sent praise to God in deep brazen tones.

The bells were cast in the churchyard of the abbey and made of the finest metal that could be had, by the most skilful smiths that could be found.

Now, in those days there were pirates sailing up and down the sea along the coasts, robbing and plundering wherever they could find prey. What they liked best to find was an abbey, for some of the abbeys had great wealth because of the gifts made to them of money and golden vessels and jewelled cups and the like.

The abbey of the glen was one of the richest, for it had prospered greatly in the long years that had passed since the first monks came. Men of wealth and great standing had sent their sons to be schooled there and had paid generously for the service, and many were the priceless gifts that had been given to the abbey.

The monks of all abbeys lived in terror of the pirates, and those of the abbey of the glen feared them no less than the rest. Still, the abbey was well hidden and hardly to be seen from the sea, for the stones with which it had been built were the same colour as the grey rocks of the glen. Besides that, great trees grew

between the abbey and the sea, and screened it with
their wide-spreading branches.

The wicked pirates might never have found the
abbey at all, had it not been for one young lay brother.

The young lay brother loved the sweet-singing
bells so dearly that he would have sent their voices
to Heaven in praise every hour of day and night. But
when it was known that the pirates were nearby, it was
forbidden that anyone should ring the bells lest the
pirates hear and come down upon the abbey to raid it.
It was always the pirates' way to seek for an abbey by
day, and when they had found where it was, they
would steal on it by night and take it by surprise.

As happens very often, temptation was too great for
the young lay brother. For a while he fought against it
and only laid his hand lovingly but lightly on the bell
ropes when he passed by during the forbidden times.
But one evening as he was on his way to vespers, he
not only laid his hand upon the ropes but, thinking a
very little peal would be scarcely heard, he gently
pulled the rope of the smallest bell.

Clear and silvery, one chiming note rang out, down
to the shore and across the waters of the sea. But
hidden from the abbey round a point of rock a pirate
ship lay moored, to take on fresh water. The silver
note came to the ears of the captain of the pirate ship,
who knew at once that the sound of a bell meant there
was an abbey somewhere near.

As soon as they had finished storing the water in
the ship, the captain sent out a spy to find where the
abbey lay. Then they waited in hiding, until the moon
rose and lit the way, and soon after, the pirates were
battering at the gates of the abbey.

The abbot knew by the fury of the attack that pirates

were upon them. He ordered the monks and their pupils to carry away the chests of the abbey treasures, and flee by a small door at the side to the caves of the glen where the pirates would not think to seek for them. He stayed back himself to gather the cross and the vessels from the altar. A brave man was that abbot, for he had no more than reached the little side door with the rood and the holy vessels gathered into the skirts of his robe when the pirates broke down the gates and rushed into the abbey grounds. He heard their shouts of rage when they found the abbey deserted and the treasure not to be found. He heard their cries of disappointment at finding so little plunder, and then he heard them shout that they would have the bells since there was naught else worth the taking.

When the abbot heard they were going to take the bells that the people had cast and given the abbey for love, he forgot his own danger. He turned at the door and, holding high the cross he had saved from the altar, he called the wrath of God down upon them all.

'Have the bells!' he cried at the end. 'Take them if you will! But they will give you neither profit nor good.'

The pirates neither saw the abbot nor heard a word of his curse. Up in the bell tower they were, tearing loose the bells and hauling them down the ladder from the bell loft with great clamour and noise.

So the abbot went away from the abbey and made his way up the glen in safety.

When the pirates had the bells all down, they rejoiced to have such a great pile of metal of a quality so fine and pure. They were sure of getting a good price for it when they got it to the foreign ports where they'd offer the bells for sale. They carried them off to their

143

ship, but before they left they set fire to the abbey.

When they were back on their ship again, they stored the bells in the hold and then they prepared to set sail. The captain of the pirates looked back at the burning abbey and at the sky, red with dancing flames that seemed to reach clear to the moon. He roared with laughter and vowed that he'd never set a grander bonfire nor found loot more to his liking.

But while he stood there looking and laughing, the stolen bells in the hold began to peal. First rang the silver-tongued smallest bell. Then, one by one the others joined in, and last of all the great bell boomed out its deep-toned song. And the peal they pealed was the death knell!

Then the pirate crew came running to the captain. Near-deafened they were by the sound of the bells. They screamed out to the captain that something was amiss with the ship, for the sails were all set and the wind was stiff and the seas running free, but the sails would not fill and the ship would not move at all. The bells were accursed, they shouted.

So then they ran to open the hold and throw the bells into the sea. But before the crew could lay hand upon the hatches, they flew open. There lay the bells rolling gently from side to side and tolling as they rolled. Before the terrified pirates' eyes the bells began to increase in size, growing bigger and bigger and bigger. The timbers of the ship creaked and strained, but the bells kept on growing until at last the ship could contain them no longer. With a great wild noise of crashing masts and breaking beams, the ship flew apart, and down to the bottom of the sea went pirates, bells and all.

The monks who had been drawn from their caves at

the sound of their bells, watched in wonder. They could
see the ship by the light of the flames and the moon.
When the ship went down, they grieved at the fate of
the bells they loved so well. But they said to each other
that the hand of God is ever heavy upon evil-doers.

Now when the people of the countryside saw the
flames in the sky, they rushed to the abbey, fearing that
all the monks were dead. Great was the joy of the
people when they found them safe and unharmed. In
thanksgiving for their safety, they built the monks a
new chapel and abbey and had a new peal of bells cast,
as fine as the lost ones.

There were five of them, just as there had been
before, and all were the same as before, from the
silver-tongued smallest bell to the brazen-tongued
largest bell of all. And it is a strange queer thing that
whenever the new bells were pealed and sent their
noble tones over the waters of the sea, there came back
from the sea an answering peal. There are those who
will tell you 'tis only some odd sort of echo, but the
truth of it is that it is the drowned bells the pirates
stole, ringing back from the bottom of the sea. Even
to this day you can hear them if you listen.

The Lass that Couldn't be Frighted

THERE ONCE was a lass and naught could ever give her a fright! At least, that was what folks said about her.

She lived all alone on a bit of a farm that stood in the forest. Her mother died when she was a wee thing, and her father — the poor man — was never much use to her, he being more often found at the inn, in the village nearby, than at home or at work. Besides that, one day he just wandered away somewhere, and wherever it was he went he never came back.

When it was plain to see he was gone for good, folks told her she'd best come down to live in the village, seeing she had no kin of her own to take her in.

'But why should I?' she asked. 'I'm very well as I am.'

'Lawks!' said the folks. 'And are you not afraid to bide by yourself in that lonesome place? 'Tis enough to fright the soul out of a body!'

'Think of all the wild beasts about!' they said.

'Hoots!' said she. 'Well you know there are no wild beasts in the forest, barring a hart or happen a hare after the kail or a wee fox trying for the hen run.'

But the cottagers were awful uneasy about her. For you never could tell! The forest was big and dark. Anything could be in it — and there might be worse things abroad by night than wild beasties.

'What then?' she asked.

They looked to the left and they looked to the right, and then they put their heads close to hers and whispered, '*The Wee People!*'

'Och!' laughed she. 'Goblins and ghaisties and such like! Goodwife's tales to scare the bairns with!'

They were horrified at that. Did she not believe in the Wee Folks? Well, she wouldn't say 'aye,' nor would she say 'nay' to that. But what she did say was, that if there were any of them, why she didn't mind them at all.

So they gave up talking to her about it, but what they said to each other was that she was uncommon brave for a lassie. And that's how the story came about that she was a lassie that couldn't be frighted.

The strange thing was that it was true. With her dog and her cat she was well able to keep the hares from her garden and the foxes from her hens. And if a bear had come to rob her hives (though, of course, there were none in the forest) she'd just have twisted his ear and spatted him back to the forest with the flat of her hand to his backside. As for the fairies — well, if there were any about let them keep to their ways and she'd keep to hers.

With her house and her garden and her cow and her two sheep and her hens and her beehives she was well fixed, and with her dog and her cat for company what more could she ask?

True, she seldom saw money from one year's end to the other, but the things from her wee farm that she had over what she needed for her own use she could trade in at the shop in the village for whatever she couldn't raise or make for herself. So what good would money be to her, the way things were? And being contented, she was as happy as the day is long.

Then one day one of the lads from the village looked at her, and he saw that she was the bonniest lass in all the countryside. Then, having taken one look he took another, and saw that she had come to an age when she might well think of getting married. He went and told a friend or two and those took the word of it to one or two more, and in no time all the lads for miles around were clustered at her gate like bees in a swarm, all buzzing round at her to make her pick one of them to wed. All the lads but one, that is, and that one was Wully the weaver's son, who had a croft on the hillside over against the forest. When one of the lads told him she was awful bonny he said, aye he'd known that for long. And when they said she was old enough to wed he said that he knew that, too. And when they asked if he wasn't going to be wooing her the lads all thought he was plain daft, for he said, nay he thought he'd just bide his time, and up he climbed to his croft and tended his sheep.

Little good came to the ones who stayed to woo her, for she wouldn't have any of them.

'Why should I?' she asked them.

To protect her? Well, she hadn't had trouble doing that for herself. Besides, she had her dog.

For money? Well, that she did not want nor need.

For love? And she only laughed, and said that when the lad she could fancy came along she'd give that her consideration. But for the present, she'd stay as she was.

So at last all the lads were so discouraged that they left her to look elsewhere, which did not displease her at all.

The lads who had given up trying to win her told

Wully the weaver's son that maybe he'd done well not to waste his time on such a headstrong lassie, and besides it wasn't natural for a lass not to be afraid of aught. But all Wully said was, 'Och, we'll see then,' and went on tending his sheep.

So days went by and weeks went by, and then one evening the lassie went to the meal bin to fetch herself some meal to make some bannocks for her supper.

'There now!' she said. 'When I fill the bowl the bin will be empty!' and she scraped and scraped at the bottom of the bin. 'There'll be no oatmeal for the porridge in the morn,' said she.

So she made up her mind that as soon as she'd had her supper she'd take a sack of oats to have it ground at Hughie the miller's mill.

When she'd baked her bannocks and eaten them she went to the shed and filled a sack with oats, and taking it on her arm off she set for the mill. 'Twas a fine warm night, so she enjoyed the walk, but when she got to the mill the house beside it was dark and the mill shut tight, for the miller and all his family had gone off somewhere for a visit and there was nobody at home to grind her oats for her.

She set her sack on the sill of the house and sat herself down beside of it, to consider what she was to do.

Lachie the miller had a mill, too, but it lay over on the edge of the next village, a long ways off. It would be far to go, but she could think of nothing better to do if she was going to have porridge in the morning. So up she got and took up her bag of oats, and off she went again.

When she left Hughie's mill dusk was closing in, and when she got to Lachie's mill the night was as

dark as the inside of one of the caves of Cruachan.
Lachie's mill was idle and still and the door was locked,
but that did not trouble her, for the house of the miller,
over the way, showed a light. So she went up to the
house and clackit at the door.

The miller came to the door and stood there staring
at her.

'I've brought you a bag of oats to be ground at the
mill,' said the lass. And when the miller said nothing
she added civilly, ' 'Tis sorry I am to trouble you so
late, but I've no meal in the house at all against the
morn.'

'I'll grind no meal in the mill tonight,' said the
miller then. 'Come back on the morrow's morn.'

But the lass wasn't going to be put off that way.
'I'm telling you I've no meal in the house for the
morning's porridge!' she said impatiently.

'Come back fasting then,' said the miller, 'for I'll
grind no meal tonight!'

'Well then, give me the key to the mill,' the lass told
him, 'and I'll grind my meal myself!'

'Woman!' roared the miller, 'I will not grind your
meal nor will I give you the key! For when anyone
grinds grain in the mill o' nights a great ugly goblin
comes up through the floor and steals the grain and
beats him black and blue!'

'Hoots! Toots! to your goblin!' the lass shouted
back at him. 'I'll grind my grain, goblin or no goblin!
Miller, give me the key!'

So determined was she that the miller fetched the
key, but he would not give it to her until he had called
his wife and all in his house to witness that he was not
to blame whatever happened to her.

Then she took the key, and the miller's wife lit a

lanthorn and gave it to her, to light her so that she could see to grind her meal.

The lass went off to the mill and unlocked the door. She opened it and looked all about, but there was nothing there. So she went and opened the water into the race, and the mill wheel began to turn round. Clack! Clack! Whish! Clack! Clack! Whish! Clack! Clack! Whish! went the mill wheel.

So then she poured the grain into the hopper and sat herself down to rest a minute while the grain went through, for the long walk had tired her a little and she still had to walk back. But it was not long till the meal was through, so she let it pour out into her sack. When all her meal was in the sack she knotted the top, and she said to herself said she, 'Well! There's nothing here to fash myself about!'

And just then up through the floor rose a great ugly goblin! He had a big black club in one hand and he stretched the other one out to grab her sack of meal!

'No you don't!' shrieked the lass, for the first thought in her mind was losing her morning's porridge. So she snatched the club from the goblin's hand and off she took after him.

Now the goblin had met many a man in that mill by night, but never before in all his days had he met a woman like the lass. He didn't know just what to do, for it was a new thing entirely, especially since she had hold of his club. A goblin's wits are never very fast at working so he just backed away.

The lass came after and banged the goblin over his ugly head with the big black club. Into the corners and out again she drove him, and round and round the mill, and sometimes she hit the goblin and sometimes she hit the wall, but all of it made a fearful sort of a racket.

The miller slammed the house door to and he and his wife and all the household put their hands up over their ears to shut out the terrible din!

And then the goblin came up alongside the hopper where the grain was poured down. Against the hopper there was a big oaken bar. The goblin just turned his back for a minute so as to take up the bar, and the lass came up close and planted her foot in the middle of the goblin's back and gave it a monstrous shove. Into the hopper headfirst went the goblin, and the lass turned the mill wheel on!

So there was the goblin between the mill stones, going round and round and round and round! It didn't kill him, for nothing can kill a goblin, but it hurt him awful bad.

'O-o-o-o-o-o-ow!' shrieked the goblin. 'Let me out! Let me out! Let me out!' And he shrieked so loud it all but lifted the roof clear off the mill. The miller and his wife and all were that frighted that they crept under their beds and pulled their pillows down tight over their ears. But even then they could hear the noise.

'Let me out!' screamed the goblin.

'Stay down there!' called the lass, as she wiped her face and settled her skirts, for the fight had been a hot one. ' 'Twill do you good!'

'Och, let me out,' begged the goblin, 'and I promise you I'll go away and bother you no more.'

'You will, then?' asked the lass.

'I promise you I will,' said the goblin.

'Well that's worth considering,' said the lass.

She shut off the water. The mill wheel stopped

turning, the goblin stopped screeching, and all was quiet. But the goblin didn't come up. So the lass reached down, and she caught hold of him by the neck, and she drew him up out of the hopper.

Never was there seen, since the beginning of time, such a terrible used-up goblin. He said not one word, but limped out through the door of the mill and never again was he seen or heard of in those parts.

The lass shouldered her sack of meal and took the goblin's club under her arm and the key and the lanthorn in her hand. She went out of the mill and locked the door and went across to the miller's house. She knocked on the door there for a long, long time before the miller got brave enough to open it. But at last he crept down the stairs and opened it a wee crack.

'Here's your lanthorn and here's your key,' said the lass. 'I've ground my meal and I've got rid of your goblin for you. And now I'm going home!' And home she did go, with the club and the sack of meal.

By the time she'd made her porridge in the morn the news was all over the village about how she'd driven the goblin out of Lachie's mill.

Lachie had risen early and told the tale all over the countryside. It was at the blacksmith's shop, where he'd stopped in to get a bit of mending done, that Wully the weaver's son heard about it. His heart ached inside of him, for he had been thinking that maybe the lass would change her mind someday about wanting a man to fend for her, and maybe if she did, he'd be that man. But that was when her being afraid of naught was just a lot of talk. But what he'd heard at the blacksmith's shop looked like proof that the talk was true enough.

'Och,' he said sadly, ' 'tis sure she'll never be needing me now.' He started up the road very slowly, one foot then t'other. But when he came where the road went into the forest, he heard something that made the hairs of his head stand straight up and he began to run. Because it was the lass's voice, and she was screaming at the top of it! Maybe it wasn't as loud as the goblin screamed, but it was close to that.

'It must be a band of robbers has got after her, and they're killing her,' panted Wully, as he raced up the road towards her farm.

He came to her dooryard and rushed in, picking up a big club that lay by the gate as he ran.

He threw the door open and took a stand, ready to battle whoever was there, no matter how many! And then he stopped!

There was the lass, standing upon the table between the porridge bowl and the bowl of milk, holding her skirts to her knees and screaming for help with her eyes tight shut! And playing around on the floor below was a wee brown mousie.

Wully set the club down and leaned against the doorpost. He let her scream a little bit longer and then he said, 'They've been telling me you're the lassie that nothing could fright.'

The lass opened her eyes and cried to him, 'Och Wully, put the beastie out! The dog's gone into the woods and the cat's off in the fields, and there's nobody here can save me but you!'

'Happen you need a man to take care of you after all,' said Wully.

'Happen I do!' sighed the lass.

So he took the broom from behind the door, and he drove the wee beastie out of the house.

Then he jumped the lass down from the table, and

took her in his arms and kissed her. 'We'll be married o' Sunday,' said Wully.

'Aye,' said the lass, and she laid her head on his shoulder as if that was where it belonged.

So married they were, and happily, too. But whenever she had a bit too much to say for herself, Wully would just say 'mousie!' And then she'd grow rosy red and hang down her head, and have no more to say. With all so well understood between them 'tis no wonder that they lived happily ever after.

The Fisherlad and the Mermaid's Ring

ONCE THERE was a lad who offered his heart to a bonny lass. She smiled at him kindly and spoke to him softly, but she would not have his heart at all, because she loved somebody else. So she told the lad that he must take his heart and find another lass to give it to.

'It will be a long long day and I shall go a long long way ere I do that!' said he. And he stamped away from her, sure that he'd never find a lass that could ever take her place.

He was a fisherman, but when she would not have him, he would go no more to the shore with the other lads, lest they put shame upon him for having misgiven his heart. So he took up his nets and sailed away, until he came to a cove where no one save himself ever came. There on the shore he built himself a hut to bide in. From the cove he sailed each day alone to set his nets and draw up his fish. The fish he caught he took to market at a port where he was a stranger, for he would not show his face again in a place where he was known.

So day in and day out he set his nets and drew up his fish and nursed his sorrow. When he had been away for a year and a day, as he drew up his nets from the sea he saw there was something strange among the fish in one of them. He thought at first that it was only a great fish, but when he had the net clear of the water he looked closer. Then he saw that it was a mermaid.

Quick as a wink he caught it by the arm through the mesh of the net and, though it struggled hard, he held it fast. He tipped the fish out, but he kept hold of the mermaid all the while. Then he wrapped the folds of the net tight about it so that it wouldn't be getting away from him. He set the creature up before him on one of the thwarts of the boat, and looked it over to see what it was like. What he saw was a lass like any other lass as far down as her waist. But from there she was like a fish, all covered with shining bright scales.

The mermaid set to weeping and begged him to let her go, but the fisherman shook his head. 'Nay, I'll not do that!' he said.

'On the floor of the sea are many great ships that have foundered in the storms,' the mermaid said. 'Let me go and I'll fetch you a kist of gold from one of them.'

'What good is gold to me?' asked the fisherman. ' 'Twill not give me what I want.'

'My father is one of the kings of the sea,' said the mermaid. 'His castle is made of the pearls of the sea and he has rich treasures of precious gems. Set me free and he will send you a ransom of gold from his store.'

'What good are jewels to me? They will not give me what I want,' said the lad.

'What is it that you want then?' asked the mermaid.

'I want the lass I love best in all the world,' said the lad. 'She's not to be had for gold nor jewels, nor will a true heart win her. For I offered her my own and she would not take it. But there's not a lass her equal in all the weary world.'

'What is she like then that makes her so different?'

'She has two blue eyes,' said the lad.

'So has many another lass,' said the mermaid.

'But not the like of hers,' said he.

The mermaid smiled. 'And what more?' she asked.

'She has hair the gold of the midday sun,' said the lad.

'So has many another lass,' said the mermaid.

'But not the like of hers,' said he.

'Eyes of blue and golden hair,' said the mermaid. 'Well — and what more?'

'She is tall and straight and supple as a young ash tree,' said the lad.

'So is many another lass,' said the mermaid. 'To me she does not seem greatly different. But what more?'

'Och, what does it matter?' cried the lad. 'What I want above all in the world is the lass I love and if I can't have her, I want naught else!'

'The lass you love,' said the mermaid thoughtfully. 'I think we could give you even that, if you will but let me go free.'

'Nay,' said the lad. 'You'll ne'er do that. I doubt that she'll be wedded by now.'

'She'll not be,' promised the mermaid. 'But you will have to come with me to my father. He is the one who can give you what you wish. Do you dare come with me into the sea?'

'I dare!' said the lad. Hope had cast out all fear from his heart.

So he cut the net from the mermaid and she took him by the hand and drew him down under the sea to her father's castle.

The sea king sat on a throne of pearl in his great hall.

He greeted his daughter with joy, for the fishes had brought him word that she had been caught in the fisherlad's net. When his daughter told him her story, he was not pleased that she should be bargained for like a catch of fish in the market. But a promise was a promise and her word was as good as his own. Besides, she was so dear to him and he was so glad to have her safe that he was ready to give the lad what he asked.

'So, you want the lass you love best in all the world?' said the sea king. 'Well! 'Twill take a bit of doing to get you that. Could you bear to wait a bit longer if you got what you wanted in the end?'

'It could be borne,' the lad said, 'if it had to be.'

'For another year and a day,' said the sea king, 'you must bide in your cove and do as you have done day in and night out. Though the time seem long and you grow weary of waiting, 'tis what you must do.'

'I'll do so then!' said the lad.

Then the sea king sent for a casket of jewels, and from it he took a ring of gold all set round with pearls.

'You did well,' said the king, 'to refuse to take gold or jewels for my daughter's freedom, for neither of them ever gives true happiness. When the year and the day are over, if you go to the lass you love best in all the world, you'll find her waiting for you. Take this ring and keep it carefully, and when you find her, put it on her finger and wed her with it.'

The lad took the ring and thanked the king for it. Then the king sent a great fish to carry him back to his cove. There, everything was just as he left it except that his boat was drawn up on the shore. The sails were furled and the nets within it were mended where he had cut them. The sea king had taken care of all that, too.

The lad went up to his hut and laid off his wet clothes to dry. The ring he laid on the chimney shelf against the time when he'd be needing it.

So he started out to serve his time, setting his nets and drawing up his fish and taking them to be sold. It was not sorrow that he nursed now, but hope for the day when he'd be claiming his own true love.

No more than a week had gone by when he came home one night in the gloaming, and as he drew his boat up out of the sea, he saw what he took to be a heap of seaweed lying upon the stone of his doorstep. He wondered how it came to be there, and hurried up from the shore to see.

When he got there, he found that it was not sea-weed, but a lass who crouched on the doorstone. Her face was hidden in her lap and her hair streamed down around her. It was her hair that he had taken for sea-weed because it was brown and so thick and long that it covered her to the ground.

When she heard his footstep, she sat up and her hair fell away from her face. Then he saw that her face was wet and her eyes were red with weeping. He was in no mood for anybody's troubles but his own, so he asked her roughly, 'What are you doing here?'

'I've run off from my father's house,' she told him. 'There's a new stepmother there and she no older than myself. There's no place for me there because she can't abide me, and I came away lest she do me some harm.'

'Then you'd best run back again,' said the lad. 'For there's no place for you here, either.'

'Och, do not drive me away,' begged the lass. 'I've wandered many a weary mile and found no place where they'd take me in. Let me stay, and I'll keep your house and cook your food and do for you all I can.'

'I can do for myself,' said the lad.

At that the lass burst into tears again. 'I can go no farther,' she wept in despair. 'If I cannot bide here, I must just go down and jump into the sea!'

The lad could no longer bear the sight and sound of her grief. His heart filled with pity for her and he said more gently, 'Whisht, lass! Bide here then, if you like. Only keep out of my way.'

So she stayed. True to her word, she kept the house and kept it as bright and shining as a new pin — what there was of it. And as he had commanded, she kept out of his way. The only times he saw her at all were when she served him his meals. She kept herself back in a corner even then, and came forward only to fill his plate again or give him something he was looking about for. When she ate or where she stayed for the rest of the time, he never thought to ask.

So it went on for a week or two, with him at his fishing and her at her housework, and he saw and heard so little of her 'twas as if she wasn't there.

Then, one night as he was coming up from his boat, he thought it was a foolish sort of thing for two human souls to bide in one house and hold so little converse together. So he went in and he said, 'Set yourself a place on the table across from me, lass, and eat your supper like a Christian!' and so she did.

After they had sat together at meals for a week or two, they began to find words to say to each other. Soon they knew all there was to know about each other. He said that she'd done well to leave her father's house, and she said the blue eyes and golden hair and the grace of his true love must be the wonder of the world!

So, since they were so well agreed, both of them were content.

About that time, she took to coming down to the shore of an evening to help him beach the boat and spread the nets. She was only a wee thing, and it gave him a laugh to see her lay hold of the big boat. But for all that, she was sturdy, so her help was worth something to him. He was glad enough to have it when he came in tired after the day's work.

It came to his mind once, as she ran up the path before him to make sure his supper'd be good and hot, that she was bonny enough in her own way. To be sure, there was naught of the blue and gold of his true love about her and she'd never be reminding a man of a young ash tree. She was as brown of skin and hair and eye as an autumn hazel nut, and so small you'd be taking her for a bairn at first sight. But for all that, she was neatly made, and she was as light on her feet as a dry leaf borne on the wind.

Before he knew it, half of the days of his time were over. She was the one who told him so, for she had worked it out on a chart she'd made, marking the days off one by one. It was clever of her, he said, for he'd have never thought of doing such a thing himself.

Now that they were so well acquainted, she began to grow bolder. She never could be happy unless she was busying herself with something or other. It wasn't enough that the house was tidy and clean. First, it was flowers that she brought from the fields to plant by the house wall. Then it was a wild rose that she trained to twine above the door. Now, she began to ask him to fetch things from the town where he sold his fish. He must bring glass for the window holes to keep the weather out. He grumbled a bit, but he brought the glass and made frames for it too, and fitted the windows into their places in the wall.

Then she said the room was too bare, so he must fetch her a bit of stuff for her to be making curtains of. He told her they'd been getting along well enough before they ever had either glass or curtains for the windows. But she only said that was then and this was now, and for him to be off because she had work to do even if he didn't.

Then he must bring some white to wash the walls with inside, for the room was too dreary and dark. What with one thing and another, he complained that she wore him out and kept his pocket light.

It was about this time that he found out that she'd been laying a pallet in the shed to sleep on of nights among the oars and the fishing gear. He'd never given a thought to where she slept, but when he found it out, he took steps to change it. He laid off from his fishing for a time and got busy at it.

When she saw him about the place, measuring and hauling stone and hacking at this and that, she came out to watch him. 'What will you be at now?' she asked.

'I'm building a room to the house,' said he.

'Whatever for?' said she.

'For you to have a place for yourself,' he told her. ' 'Tisn't seemly that you should be sleeping amongst the bait and the boat gear.'

'Och!' said she and went back into the house. But he heard her singing as she went about her work, and it came to his mind that his mother used to do the same.

So the days slipped by. Soon there were a wheen of them marked off on the lass's chart and but a few days left to be marked.

The house had a but and a ben with glass in the windows of both of the rooms and curtains to all of the windows, as well as glass. The walls were white as milk, and there was a drugget on the floor that the lass had made herself, and a hearth with a hob that the lad had built. There was a fire on the hearth and a shining kettle singing on the hob. And on the shelf above the fire was a clock that the lad had brought from the town, ticking busily beside the sea king's pearl ring.

One day the lad came in and caught the lass with the ring upon her finger. She was holding up her hand and looking at the ring.

'What are you doing there?' he asked sharply.

She jumped and looked frighted. 'Och!' said she. 'I was just having a look at it!'

'Well, put it away and do not do so again!' he ordered, going on out to the shed to put his gear away.

'Till you give me leave,' she said softly to his back. But he didn't hear her. She slipped the ring from her finger and laid it back in its place on the shelf by the clock.

When he came back she said to him, 'I'll soon be leaving here.'

'You will!' said he. 'Why will you then?'

'The year and the day will soon be up and you'll be going to fetch your own true love,' she told him.

'You'd best stay here,' said the lad.

'Och, I'd not be liking to do that,' she said.

'Where can you go then?' he asked her.

'Back to my father's house,' said she.

'Are you not afraid to go back there?' he asked.

'Nay! I'm a lot older now,' said she. 'I can look after myself.'

'A lot older!' he scoffed. ' 'Tis but a year that's gone by and hardly that!'

'Happen I'm a lot wiser then,' said the lass. 'I'll go there anyway.'

So he said no more about it, nor did she.

But a few days later she rose at day's dawning and made herself a packet of all she had of her own in the world. There was little enough to take. Just her comb and an apron or two she'd made for herself, a knot of ribbon and a kerchief he'd brought her from the town, and her nightshift. When she'd packed them all, she took the bundle under her arm and laid her shawl over her shoulders. Then she went out to the lad. She took the chart from the shelf behind the clock and laid it before him where he sat at the table. And she marked the last days off.

'All of the days of your waiting are over today,' said she. 'You'll be going to claim your own true love tomorrow. So I'll wish you well and bid you farewell!'

Then she walked past him and out of the house.

He sat there for a long while staring at the door through which she had gone, like a man who has heard something but not believed his ears. When he jumped up at last and went to the door to look after her, she was out of sight.

The lad went back and sat down again in the place where he'd been sitting when she went away. All that day he did not go out in his boat nor move from his chair. He thought over all the days that had gone by since the day he caught the mermaid in his net. It took him all the hours of the day to do it. Then he went to bed.

The next morning he got up at break of dawn and dressed himself in the best he had. He took the sea king's ring from the shelf and tucked it into his pocket, and started off to claim his own true love.

But it wasn't down to his boat he went, to sail back home. Instead, he turned away from the sea, and walked inland the same way the lass had gone the day before.

She was walking in her father's garden when she saw him coming up the road. When he got up to her and spoke to her, she turned red and white by turns. But she spoke right up to him.

'I thought you had gone to claim your own true love,' said she.

'I have so!' said he. 'That's what I'm doing here!' And he took the sea king's ring from his pocket and held it out to her.

'Will you have it?' he asked her. 'And me with it, of course!'

'If you give me leave!' said she. And she took the ring from his hand and slipped it on her finger.

So they were wed and a grand time it was to be sure! Everyone danced until they could dance no more. Then when they'd rested a while they started in all over again. Even the new young stepmother danced at the lass's wedding and was glad to do it, for the two of them had made it up and were good friends in the end.

When it was all over, the lad took the lass back to his own village. He was that proud of her that he wanted them to have a look at her. Whom should he meet there but his old love! Her eyes were as blue and her hair was as gold, and she was as straight and tall and slim as ever. But she didn't look any different to him now from a lot of other blue-eyed, yellow-haired lasses he'd met in his life.

Then he tucked his wee brown bride under his arm, and took her back to the house on the shore of the cove, which was where both of them wanted to be.

The eve of the day they got there they walked down to the shore, and who should they find there sitting on a rock out in the water but the mermaid.

'Did you get your own true love?' the mermaid asked of the lad.

'I did so!' said the lad. 'And here she is!'

The mermaid took a look at the lass. 'Her eyes are not blue,' said she.

'They are not,' the lad agreed.

'And she has not golden hair,' the mermaid said.

'She has not,' said the lad.

'And I should call her neither slim nor tall,' the mermaid said.

'Nay. She's a wee thing and perhaps a bit on the plump side,' said the lad. 'But she is the one I love the best of all.'

'Well then,' said the mermaid, 'you'll not be saying we did not give you what you asked for.' And at that she dived off the rock and into the sea, and that was the last they ever saw of her.

But they never forgot her. Because they knew it was from her and her father, the sea king, that the lad had got his own true love and all the happiness that came with her.

Spin, Weave, Wear

THERE WAS a lass of Kintiemuir once, and she was a grand hand at spinning and weaving and sewing, and she was awful bonnie besides.

She was the only daughter of a well-off farmer, and as there was only herself and her father at home she looked after him and kept his house and kept her eye on the maids in the dairy.

He was so proud of her and she was so dear to him that he wouldn't have any other father's child praised above her. And as he was a great one for talking, sometimes he'd let his tongue run away with him and say more than he meant.

One day he went over to another town to see about some cattle he heard was going for sale there. And after the sales were over he sat down to dinner at the inn with a lot of other farmers who had come to town too.

The dinner was a good one, and most of the farmers were pleased with the deals they'd made, so they didn't hurry home, but sat there, talking, at the table.

Well, they talked about one thing then another, and at last they began to talk about their lads and lasses at home. Not boasting they weren't, to be sure, but each giving his own lad or lass their due.

One farmer said his lass, maybe, wasn't the bonniest ever seen, though she was bonny enough to have her choice of the lads. But she was not likely to find her match when it came to baking and cooking, and the laird's cook herself had agreed to that.

Another farmer's lad was maybe a little too scrawny and undersized ever to make much of a farmer, but, losh, he was the lad for learning. Always his nose in a book, he had. He knew more now than the Dominie himself, so his mother and himself had decided they'd make him into a minister.

And so it went, with one father's lass doing one thing and another's lad doing another, all better than anyone ever had heard of anywhere!

The farmer of Kintiemuir sat there listening, and the more he listened, the madder he got inside, to think any of them would try to claim a bairn who could do better than his own lass at home!

So when it came to his turn he said, easy and quiet-like, as if it didn't matter much, 'Och, my lass is none so bad. She's awful bonny, to be sure, but that doesn't count at all, against what she can do. For she can spin in the morning, and weave in the afternoon, and sew in the evening, and when you rise from your bed in the morn your new clothes is all laid out ready for you to wear!'

All the farmers gawped at him, for they'd ne'er heard the like! And when they went away after dinner all they could talk about was the wonderful ways of the lass of Kintiemuir.

The farmer went home and told his daughter what he'd said.

'Och, now,' said she, 'you ne'er should have said that, for you know there's no truth in it!' But she smiled at him lovingly, because she knew it was his pride and his love that made him tell such a terrible big fib. And then she put it out of her mind, not being the sort to fret over what was too late to mend.

But that sort of news travels faster by word of mouth than ever the king's messengers could carry it. In no time at all everybody the length and breadth of Scotland had heard of the lass, and the tales lost naught in the telling!

At last it reached the ear of the king in his great castle, and as things were dull in the place at the time he sent for the lass to come there and try her skill against any of the lasses in the land who thought they might do as well as she could.

When the summons came that she was to come to the court for the match by the end of the second fortnight to come, the lass couldn't think what she was ever going to do about it all!

Being one for thinking and not for weeping she sat down by the fire to see what she could do about it. Her father was about somewhere on the farm with the men, but there was no need to worrit him about it.

To the court she must go, since the king himself had sent for her. But what was she going to do when she got there? She knew, as sure as black is black and white is white, that she could not spin thread and weave cloth and sew garments all in one day. The only other way out would be to tell the king the truth — that her father had told a lie because he loved her so much and was so proud of her. Of course, she couldn't shame her father so, and besides the king might be angry and throw the poor dearie into prison for telling such a fib.

As she sat there by the fire by herself, 'Och, father,' she sighed, 'you meant no harm, but just see the pickle you've got us in!'

She couldn't shame her father, and she couldn't do

what he said she could, and if there was a third way out she didn't know what it was.

'There's no way out at all,' said she, mournfully.

'Happen there is!' said her big black cat, who sat watching her from t'other side of the hearth.

The lass jumped, and she stared at her cat. 'Is it yourself that's talking, Tom?' she asked, not believing her ears.

'Och, aye,' said the cat, and he added carelessly, 'I can do so, if there's aught I'm caring to say. And anyone I'm caring to say it to.'

'Oh,' said the lass.

'Well,' said the cat, 'this is a time for talking.'

'There's naught to say,' said the lass. 'I've mulled it o'er and o'er and I cannot do it.'

'Well then,' said the cat wisely, 'you must be helped.'

The lass looked at the cat and smiled. 'How could you help me, Tom?' she asked.

'Not me,' said the cat hastily, 'but there might be ways.'

'How?' asked she.

'You would not like to become a witch, I doubt?' asked the cat slyly.

'I would not!' said the lass.

'Och, aye. I thought not,' said the cat with a great sigh. 'Then we'll have to see if we can get one to help us. 'Twould be easier,' he coaxed, 'to turn you into a witch and let you manage for yourself.'

'No!' said the lass.

'Well,' said the cat, resigned-like, 'every self-respecting cat has a friend or two among the witches. Open the door for me, mistress, and I'll go and see what I can do.'

She opened the door and out he leapt and in a minute was gone.

He never came back till a night and a day and another night had passed. Then in the morning early, when the lass was stirring the porridge on the back of the fire, he scratched at the door. He stalked in, with his tail lashing proudly from side to side. His fur was tangled and torn, but he had a satisfied look on his face and he grinned at her through his whiskers.

'Well?' said she.

' 'Tis done!' said he. 'And tonight is the night to settle it!'

So that night he led the lassie out on the moor. They went a long way till they came to a deep dark glen, and into the glen the black cat went and the lassie followed after.

When they came to the end of the glen they saw a wee bit of fire in the cleft ahead of them. And when they got up close they saw two old crones crouched over the fire, one on either side of it.

The cat went up boldly and greeted them. 'This is the lassie I was telling you about,' said he.

They peered at her through the smoke of the fire, but said naught.

'So then,' said the cat, 'let us get to the bargain. What will you take to lay the spell we need?'

The two witches laid their heads together and whispered to each other for a while. Then they asked, 'Is it a spell for a day or a week or a month or a year you're wanting?'

'A day or a week or a month might not be long enough,' said the lass. 'And a year might be too long. Can you not make it to last till I no longer need it?'

The two crones whispered together again, and then

one of them said, 'Aye. But it would be harder and come higher. And there would be a condition to it.'

'What will ye take for the spell?' growled the cat, who was growing impatient.

'Two new brooms that have ne'er touched ground,' said the first old witch.

'Aye,' said the lass, for she could bind brooms as well as she could weave.

'Two flasks of water that the sun has never shone upon,' said the second witch.

'Aye,' said the lass, for she knew where she'd be getting that, too.

'Two bits of silver out of a gipsy lad's pocket,' said the first witch again.

'Aye,' said the cat, for that he could take care of himself.

'Two rings of gold that was never mined or minted.'

At that the lass looked at the cat, and the cat looked at the lass, for she did not know where that could be found, nor did he, as she well knew. But before she could up and say so, the cat said, 'Aye!'

So the bargain was made, and the two witches told them to come back the next night with the things they'd promised, and then they'd get on with the spell.

On the way home the cat said, 'You get the brooms and the water on the morrow, and I'll get the silver pieces ere I come home tonight.'

'But who will get the two golden rings?' cried the lassie.

'Not I!' said the cat airily. 'You can be putting your mind to that!' And with a flip of his tail off he went, and vanished into the darkness.

When the cat got to the place where the gipsies had their camp he went about until he found a likely looking lad, sleeping on a heap of rags away from the rest of the gipsies.

The cat got busy and worked very gently until he'd chewed a hole in the gipsy lad's pocket. So slyly did the cat work, that although the gipsy stirred once or twice he never woke up at all. When the hole was big enough the cat gave the lad a scratch with one of his claws. The gipsy lad jumped up to his feet to find out what had bitten him, and all his money fell out through the hole in his pocket. While he was hunting around picking it up the cat grabbed two silver pieces in his mouth and ran off with them, and the gipsy lad none the wiser!

The next morning the lass came down early and there was the cat on the doorstep. He came into the room and jumped up on the table and there he laid down the two bits of silver he had been holding in his mouth.

'There!' said he with a yawn. 'I've been out all the night and I'm tired out, so I'm going to sleep.' He curled up in a corner near the fire and stirred no more that day.

When her father came down the lass gave him his porridge, and after he had gone out to his fields she took a hatchet and a sharp knife in her apron pocket and off she went to the forest. She hunted about until she found two straight young trees that were about the size round of a broomstick. She cut them off well above the ground with her hatchet, and then she tied them on her back so that they couldn't touch the ground.

Next she climbed high up into a beech tree, and

cut a big bundle of thin twigs with her knife, and those she tied upon her back, too. Then she went home.

When she got there she peeled the sticks and trimmed the twigs and made the brooms, binding them with new woollen yarn. From the first to the last nothing about them ever touched ground, so that much was as it should be. Next she took two stone flasks to fetch the water in. She knew where to get that, for behind the scullery there was a shed and under the floor of the shed was a well. There were no windows in the shed and the well was covered with a great flat stone, so the sun never came anywhere near the water. The lass filled the flasks and put the stoppers in, and then she took them back into the house. She laid the brooms and the silver and the flasks of water on a shelf, and now all she had to be finding was the two rings of gold — and where she'd be getting them, she did not know at all!

She sat down on a stool by the hearth to think about it, and whilst she was sitting she took down her hair and began to comb it, to tidy it. As she was combing it a hair fell from her comb and lay upon her knee. She looked at it, shining in the firelight, and thought how it looked like gold.

Then she laughed aloud. For it was gold, unmined and unminted, and just what the old witchwomen had asked for!

So she cut a few strands from her head and plaited them into rings, and bound them and wound them until they were smooth and round. Then she laid them on the shelf with the brooms and the flasks of water and the silver pieces. Now she had all that she needed.

Her father came in and she gave him his supper, and then he went to bed. When he was asleep the lass woke up the cat. She put the silver pieces and the gold rings in her pocket and tied the brooms on her back. She took a flask under each arm, and set off with the black cat to the witches' glen.

When she got there she gave the witches all she had brought. And now would they give her the magic spell?

'Not so fast!' they told her. 'Time and other things are needed to make a spell that will hold good. You'll have to fetch us what we cannot get for ourselves, since we are not able to leave this place at present.'

The black cat grumbled very loud when he heard that, but there was no help for it. They said that they could not make the spell without these things, and since they could not go and get them the lass and the cat would have to be fetching them.

'What are they then?' growled the cat.

'Three sacks of thistledown, gathered from three fields in the dark of the moon,' said the first witch.

'Three sacks of wheat straw from the parson's byre,' said the second witch.

'Three long black thorns pulled from the bush at the kirk door at the stroke of midnight,' said both of the witches together.

The next night there was no moon, so the black cat and the lass went back and forth through the fields gathering thistledown. And a terrible hard task it was in the darkness.

The night after that they went to the parson's byre and filled three sacks full of wheat straw.

The third night they went to the kirk, and right on the toll of midnight they pulled three long black thorns from the bush at the door.

Then they went back to the glen.

The witches took the thistledown and passed it through the smoke of the fire, one sackful at a time. And what they sang as they passed it through no one can ever tell, for they sang in a language only witches know. When they had finished they gave the sacks back to the lass. Two of the sacks were filled with what looked like the finest carded wool, but the third sack had flax tow in it.

'Use these for your spinning,' the witches said. 'You will spin three lots of thread, one by one, and when you put the wool on the distaff the wheel will turn of itself, and faster than mortal hand could ever turn it, and if you leave it then to itself, by the morning's end your spinning will all be done.'

Then they seized the wheat straw and threw it into a tub. They leached it and heckled it and wrung it out and combed it. Then they passed it back and forth through the smoke, while they sang their witches' song. And when they had finished they had three hanks of yarn. Two were like soft, soft wool, but the other one was like fine white linen. They gave these to the lass, too.

'You will weave three webs of cloth,' they told her. 'After you've had your dinner use these to set the warp, one by one. As soon as you thread the shuttle the loom will start to weave by itself, faster than mortal hand could ever throw the shuttle. Leave it alone, except to set the warp and thread the shuttle each time, and by the end of the afternoon your weaving will all be done.'

Then they passed the black thorns through the smoke in the same way, and when they were done, they handed the lass three shining needles.

'After you've had your supper,' said they, 'cut out

your cloth and thread your needles, and set one in each garment as it lays cut for the sewing. As soon as you set the needles to the cloth they will start to stitch, faster than mortal hand could ever sew, and by the time that midnight strikes, the garments will all be done.'

The lass started to thank them, but they stopped her.

'We told you a condition came with the spell,' they said, 'and here it is. From the time you step over the threshold of the king's castle until you return to your father's house you must not speak one word. If you do, the magic spell will be broken, and you will no longer have the power we have given you.'

Aye, the lass understood, and not a word would pass her lips. She would be sure to mind that well.

Then each of the witches slipped one of the golden rings on a finger and hung one of the stone flasks by its handle on one of the broomsticks. 'Now we can leave this place!' said they, and they each mounted a broom, and striking the broomstick with a silver piece they cried, 'Off and away!' Up they flew into the sky and soon were out of sight.

So the lass and the black cat went home, taking the witches' wares along with them.

On the day appointed the lass came to the king's castle with her father.

She had told her father nothing at all about the help she had got from the witches. All she had said was that she had it in her mind not to say a word while she was at the king's court, so he could just be doing the talking for both of them. That suited him fine, for he was overfond of talking, which will be understood, since it was his tongue that had caused all her trouble.

In all the country there had been found only three lasses who were willing to try to match the lass of Kintiemuir, although the king's heralds had gone up and down through the land proclaiming the contest, and the king had offered a prize of gold to the one who came out ahead. All the others got discouraged before they could begin when they heard what was said about the farmer's daughter.

Since the three other lasses had not yet come, the lassie and her father had to wait till they got there. There was a great crowd of lords, and ladies, and gentlemen come to see who would win, and they all liked the lassie well.

But though she would smile or nod or shake her head, not one word would she say. As for her father, he talked enough for a half a dozen, and would have made his story about her even bigger had she not kept beside him all the time with her hand on his arm to stop him when his tales flew too high. You see, he'd told it so often he'd begun to believe it himself!

Among the gentlemen was one young laird who had decided the minute she stepped in at the door that she was the one he wanted to wed. So he followed her wherever she went, and as she would not talk to him, he talked to her. Since he never could find her away from her father, the second day he asked her to marry him, in spite of the father being there. The father was willing enough, but it seemed the lass wasn't, for she only smiled and shook her head and led the old man away to the other end of the castle.

The young laird sulked for a day or two, and then the other lassies came, and the next day they were going to begin the match.

The young laird caught her as she was going up the

stairs that night and again he asked her to wed him, but again she smiled and shook her head and went away up the stairs to her bed.

So he almost decided to ride away, but then he didn't after all, for he wasn't the kind to give up so easy when he wanted her so bad.

The next morning the king's servants woke all the lassies up early, and they took each one to a separate room, high up under the roof of the castle. There was naught in each room but a spinning wheel, a loom, a table, and a chair. On the table in the room was a heap of wool and tow, and a pair of shears and a needle. Besides that there was only a tray which held the food for the day.

When the servant had gone away and left her and shut the door behind him the lass started in. She paid no attention to what was on the table for she had brought her own things with her.

She set the wool from the first bag on the distaff and at once the wheel began to turn so fast she could hardly see it. When it stopped, she took off the big ball of thread that was there and started it again. Three times she set it that morning, and when the big bell in the courtyard rang at noon she was through with the spinning and the sacks were all empty, but she had three balls of thread.

Then she took the cover off the tray and sat down at the table and ate a good dinner, making sure to leave enough of the food for supper time.

Then she covered up the tray again and brushed up the crumbs and put them out of the window for the birds.

Now she was through with her dinner, so she took the first ball of the witches' warp and set the loom.

Then she threaded the shuttle with thread from the first ball that had been spun in the morning. The minute she threaded the shuttle it jerked itself out of her hand, and the loom began to weave all by itself. Click-clack! Clack-clickety-clack! Clickety-clickety-clickety-clack! Faster and faster and faster, till her eye couldn't see the shuttle as it flew back and forth.

But as it wove the cloth took colour, where before all had been white. Three times she set the warp and threaded the shuttle that afternoon, and when the bell in the courtyard tolled for eventide she had three big webs of cloth. One was of fine dark green wool and one was the king's own tartan, but the third one was linen so fine it felt like the richest silk.

So then she sat down to her supper and ate with a good appetite. When she had finished, she piled up the dishes on the tray and laid the cover on it again, and set the tray in the hall. Then she brushed up the crumbs and threw them out of the window.

Then she was ready to get on with the work. She lit a candle to see by, for it was getting dark. Then she took up her shears and began to cut her cloth. She cut a jacket and trews from the green cloth, and a kilt from the tartan, and from the fine white linen she cut a shirt.

When she had finished with the cutting she took the witches' needles from her pocket and threaded them with some of the thread that was left over. She set a needle into each of the garments, and at once they began to stitch away, all by themselves and so fast she couldn't even see them. And when the bell in the courtyard tolled for midnight there lay upon the table a fine green coat and a pair of trews, a fine tartan kilt, and a white ruffled shirt, all so well made that the king himself could not scorn them.

The lassie took up the garments and blew out the candle, and went down to bed. She was that tired out with watching things work that she fell asleep in the middle of a yawn, and never woke till the sun was high in the morning.

She got up and dressed herself, then she rang for a servant and showed him by signs that he was to take the garments to the king. After that she went down to her breakfast.

There was nobody in the great dining hall when she got there, for the king was so delighted with the garments he had put them on at once and sent for all the court to come and see. So everyone was up with the king saying, 'Oh!' and 'Ah!' and 'Och, well now!'

But while the lassie was eating her porridge in came the young laird, and him in a terrible taking. He came right up to her where she sat at the big long table all by herself.

And he said to her, said he, 'I've asked you once and I've asked you twice and I'll ask you again, and then I'll ask no more. For if you won't wed me, I'll go away and look for somebody else! Will you have me?'

She swallowed the porridge she had in her mouth and she answered quick, 'I'll have you!' Then she dropped her spoon in her porridge bowl and cried out, 'Lawks! I've destroyed the magic spell!'

Well, then she had to tell him the whole story, but when he heard it he said he didn't mind at all. He wouldn't want his wife spinning and weaving and sewing and besides he always got his clothes from the tailor. When she saw he didn't mind then she didn't either, for the spell had lasted as long as she needed it, which was what the witches had promised.

And what about the other lassies? Well, the first one was half done, the second one was a third done, and the third one hadn't started at all, for when she saw the big heap of wool she got so discouraged that she just sat down and cried all day.

But the king was a good-natured, pleasant king, so he gave each of the three lassies a kind word and thanked them for coming, and sent them away with a fine present, and happy anyway.

Everybody agreed that the lass of Kintiemuir had fairly won the prize. The king was so pleased that he doubled the prize, which made a grand dower for the lassie to bring to her lord.

The king took such pleasure from his new clothes that the lass and her laird never told him it was all done by magic. There was nobody else could tell him, for nobody else knew but the witches and the lassie's big black cat. The witches were gone for good, and as for the big black cat — he'd stopped talking!

So the king gave the two of them a grand wedding, and all the lords and ladies and gentlemen came and danced merrily at it. After they were married, the lassie's father sold his farm and stayed at the court, for the king liked to hear him talk.

But the lassie and the laird and the big black cat rode off to the laird's castle and they all lived there happily ever after.

The Beekeeper and the Bewitched Hare

THERE WAS a lad once who lived in a cottage across the moor. He was a beekeeper, and made his living selling the honey that his bees gathered from wild flowers and heather on the moor. He lived alone, and maybe he would have been lonely if it had not been for his bees. He knew them so well, and they trusted him so completely, that he could go among them as he pleased. There were folks who said he even knew their language and what they said with their buzzing, but he said it was only the tone of it that gave him a notion of what they meant. However it was, they buzzed to him and he talked to them, and whether they understood each other or not, they were all happy together.

One evening as he stood on his doorstep in the gloaming, he heard the sound of hounds baying across the moor, and soon a hare came flying out of the heather with two dogs chasing close after.

When the hare saw him standing there, it leaped into his arms for safety's sake. The lad slipped it inside his shirt and, catching up a stick, he soon drove the dogs yelping away.

When he was sure the hounds were gone, he took the hare out to stroke it and soothe it before he let it go. It made no effort to get away from him and lay quietly in his arms, only trembling a bit from the fright it had got. When it seemed to be over its fright, he set it down and turned to go into the house to get his supper.

He thought the hare would run away into the thicket behind the house, but it followed him into the room. As he moved about getting his meal, it hopped after him. When he sat down to the table and began to eat, it leapt on to the table and sat up prettily beside his plate.

'Och!' he laughed. 'So you've come to supper, have you?' and he fed it bits from his plate. Having it close, he took a look at it and saw what he'd not noticed before. The hare's eyes were as blue as the summer skies over the moor.

'I've seen many a black-eyed hare,' said the lad, 'and I've seen pink-eyed hares with white coats in the animal-fanciers' shops, but never before have I seen a blue-eyed hare!'

It was such an odd creature that it pleased him. And since it seemed to be contented to bide with him, he decided to keep it for a pet. It was that clever and knowing. He'd ne'er seen its like before.

The next morning he took the hare out to show it to the bees. Every beekeeper knows that bees like to be told what's going on in the place where they live, and will not stay there happily unless they are. If the hare was to bide with him, the bees must know about it.

So the beekeeper carried the creature from hive to hive. 'This is my hare,' he told the bees, 'that's going to live in my house with me. So make yourselves acquainted.'

The bees flew about the hare as if they were looking it over, buzzing noisily to each other the while. The hare showed no fear of them and sat quietly till they

seemed satisfied and flew off again on their business
of honey gathering. After that, the hare followed him
about at his work and took no more harm from the
bees than he did himself.

One day as he was working among the hives with
the hare at his side, he saw an old woman coming
along the track over the moor. He thought maybe she'd
be coming to buy a comb of honey, so he stood and
waited for her.

But when she came up to him, she said naught at all
about honey. 'That's a fine-looking hare you've got,'
she said, looking down at it.

'Aye,' said he shortly. She was a stranger to him and
he did not like the looks of her. She had a sly air about
her that struck him unpleasantly.

'What will you take for her?' she asked.

'I'm not offering her for sale,' said he.

'I'll give you a bonnie piece of gold for her,' coaxed
the old woman.

'I'm not selling her!' the beekeeper said roughly.

The old woman made as if to reach down and take
up the hare. As she did so, a bee that had been hover-
ing above the hare's head gave a shrill warning buzz.
In a trice, out from the hives and in from the moor
swept a great swarm of bees. They set themselves close
together, buzzing angrily, and put themselves between
the old woman and the hare. The old woman took a
few steps back in fright, and the bees flew at her,
driving her back to the moor. She ran faster than you'd
think one so old could run and as she ran she called
back over her shoulder, 'Look well to yourself and
your hare, beekeeper!' But the bees drove her on until
she was out of the lad's sight.

Not long after, he was in the town across the moor

with some honey he had brought in to sell, for it was market day. As he stopped to pass the time of day with a man he knew, an old woman walked by. As she passed close to him he saw that it was the old body his bees had driven across the moor. When she was gone he said to the man, 'Who was that old besom just now?'

The man made a forked sign with his fingers and looked terribly frighted. 'Eist!' he said. 'Do not let her be hearing you!' Then he whispered, 'They do be saying she's a witch and has the evil eye!'

Well, maybe she was and maybe she wasn't. The beekeeper wouldn't know about that. But in any case he was going to do what she told him to do as she ran away over the moor. He'd be sure to look well to himself and his hare. He'd grown that fond of it he'd have grieved sorely had anything harmed it. He knew the bees would watch over it by day, but he took to barring the doors and the windows at night. And he kept a wary eye out for strangers coming by.

Summer went by and autumn came. The first frosts lay on the ground at morn. There were berries on the brambles for the picking. And now the bees were seeking their hives for the winter and seldom did one see more than a stray one or two, for there was no more honey to be gathered from the hedgerows or the moor.

The singing birds had flown south and, like the birds, the gipsy caravans were flitting southward too.

Few of the vans came over the moor, for although it was much shorter than the road through the towns, it was barely more than a rough track, and there were few trees to offer shelter or wood for kindling. So when the beekeeper saw a van coming across the

moor one chill October day, it surprised him. He came
out to the doorstep as it passed by in the road beyond
his gate. Being a friendly, civil soul, the beekeeper
raised a hand in greeting to the young gipsy man who
sat on the seat of the van, driving the horse. The
driver saluted with his whip as they passed by and the
lad watched him out of sight. The beekeeper went on
with his morning's work, and it wasn't till after he'd
had his dinner at noon that he had reason to come to
the door again. When he did, he saw that something
was lying in the road just past the gate. He walked
down to look at it and found that it was a sack of
grain. He knew at once that it had dropped from the
gipsy van. They'd lost it from under the wagon bed
where they usually carried such things.

'Och, they'll never miss it before they make camp
for the night,' he said. He was troubled in his mind
because he knew that it would be too late and too
dark for them to come back for it then. He did not
like to think of the poor gipsy horse going without its
evening meal. So as he could well spare the time, he
got out his market cart and hitched his own wee nag
to it, and took off after the gipsy van with the sack of
grain.

His horse was used to the road, and his cart much
lighter than their loaded van, so in an hour or so he
caught up with them. He hailed them and when they
stopped, he pulled up alongside of the van. He handed
the gipsy driver the sack of grain. 'You dropped this
in the road by my place,' he said. 'I brought it along
because I thought you might be needing it bad tonight.'

The gipsy took the sack with a look of surprise.

'I take it kindly,' said he. 'You mean to say you

fetched it all the way from the house back yonder by the moor?'

'That I did,' said the beekeeper. 'And why not?'

'We're travellers,' the gipsy told him. 'Folks don't have no use for travellers as a rule.'

'Is that a reason why a horse should be going without the dinner he's earned?' asked the lad hotly.

' 'Tis more than many would do,' the gipsy returned.

'Then they should feel shame for themselves!' the beekeeper told him, and he started to back his horse to get ready to turn and go homeward.

'Thank you kindly,' said the gipsy lad. 'I'd be glad if I —— ' then he broke off and asked, 'What's that you have?'

The beekeeper had brought the hare along with him, tucked inside his jacket. It had popped its head out and was looking at the gipsy man.

' 'Tis a hare,' said the lad, bringing it out and setting it on his knee for the gipsy to see.

'There aren't any blue-eyed hares!' said the gipsy.

'Och, now, there are indeed, for you see one here before you,' the beekeeper told him good-naturedly.

'Grandam!' shouted the gipsy. When a voice from inside the van answered, the gipsy called, 'Come out and tell this gentleman there are no blue-eyed hares.'

An old woman climbed down from the back of the van and came up to the side of the beekeeper's cart. She leaned over and looked at the hare with her old watery eyes.

' 'Tis no hare,' she said, shaking her head.

'What would it be then if not a hare?' asked the bewildered beekeeper.

The old woman took the hare from his knee and

felt it over gently. ' 'Tis a lassie, sir!' she said, ' 'Tis a lassie, and somebody's bewitched her and turned her into a hare.'

'Och!' said the lad. 'Then I can say who it was! 'Twas that old besom that came o'er the moor seeking to buy her from me. She was just trying to get her back again, and maybe she might have, only the bees wouldn't let her.'

'Are you friends with the bees?' asked the old woman.

'I love them well,' said the lad simply.

'Do you know their language?' she asked.

'Och, I can't say that I do,' the beekeeper replied. 'What they say when they are buzzing around is beyond me though they do seem to understand what I say well enough.'

'Well, if they understand you,' said the gipsy woman, ' 'twill be good enough. Now, heed what I say! The old woman will try again. She's afraid of the bees and is only waiting until she thinks they've taken to their hives for the winter. The time you have to fear most is All Hallows' Eve. That's when the witches are at the top of their power and no doubt she'll be after the hare that night.'

'Tell the gentleman what he's to do, Grandam,' said the gipsy man impatiently.

'Give me a bit of time,' the old woman said. 'I'd not like to be paying for the gentleman's kindness by telling him wrong. Go slow and go thorough. 'Tis the best way.'

She turned back to the beekeeper and said, 'When you get home, you must go to your bees and tell them you're in trouble and need their help. Tell them all that I have told you. If the bees are willing to help you when All Hallows' Eve comes round, leave your house door open, but get yourself and the hare away from the house and away from the moor as far as you can go. Tie the hare by the neck to your arm with a good stout cord and hold her fast in your arms, for when midnight comes, she'll try to get away from you because of the witch's spells. No matter how she twists and turns, you must hold on to her. It may go well and it may go ill for you. I can do no more for you.'

She handed the hare back to the lad and climbed into the van again. The driver thanked the lad again for bringing the grain, and the lad thanked him for the help he'd got from the gipsies. Then they parted and went their separate ways.

The lad went back to his house and went from hive to hive, telling his bees what the old gipsy woman had told him, and asking them for their help on All Hallows' Eve.

He could hear a great commotion in the hives. 'Bzzzzz! Bzzzzz! Bzzzzz!' said the bees, over and over again. What they were saying he didn't know at all except that they sounded uncommonly angry and upset.

When the day of All Hallows' Eve came, the bee-keeper harnessed his horse to the market cart. He tied the blue-eyed hare to his arm with a good stout cord and took her on his arm. He got into the cart, turned away from the moor and took the rough road over which the gipsy van had gone. And he left the house door open wide behind him.

On and on and on he drove, through wood and past meadow and bog and glen. Day passed and twilight fell and gave way to night. But the way was clear, for the moon was bright, so the beekeeper and blue-eyed hare went on and on and on.

Suddenly, the hare gave a spring in his arms as if it would leap from the cart. The beekeeper knew that midnight had come, so he stopped the cart and clasped the hare tight.

A cloud came over the moon and he could not see, for all was dark around him. The hare writhed and twisted and turned in his arms, and once he thought he'd lost her. But the good stout cord held fast and he got her back into his arms again, and this time she didn't get away. All at once she stopped struggling and he could feel that there was something bigger than a hare that he held in his arms. At that moment the moon shone out again and all was bright as day. What he saw in his arms was a blue-eyed lass and the bonniest he'd ever seen! There was a good stout cord around her neck and the other end of it was tied to his arm. He took the cord from her neck and from his arm, and set her beside him.

Nobody needed to tell them that the spell had been lifted from the lass. They could see that for themselves! So he took up the reins, and away they went to find a town where they could be married.

It took them a week to get back home, for they went the long way round by the market town, instead of going back the way they had come.

As they were coming through the town, whom should they meet but the man who had told the bee-keeper that the old woman was a witch. He ran up to their cart and said to the beekeeper, 'Do you mind that old woman you asked me about that I told you was a witch? Och, well! They found her the morn after All Hallows' Eve lying dead out on the moor! The strange part of it is that the doctors all say she was stung to death by bees. Now how can that be, with never a bee out at this time o' year?'

'I wouldn't know,' said the beekeeper. 'But strange things do happen.' And he smiled down at his blue-eyed wife.

Then the beekeeper and his wife drove back across the moor, and came safe home. The first thing they did was to go out to the hives and tell the bees that they were married and to thank them for their help.

And the bees said, 'Bzzz-zzz. Bzzz-zzz. Bzzz-zzz.' in a sleepy satisfied way.

The Bogles from the Howff

THERE WAS once a young doctor of learning who was sore troubled with bogles. He was the only son of an old couple to whom he had been born when they were getting along in years, and as they were determined to make a man of learning of him and had the brass to pay for it he had been little at home since he was a bit of a lad, being off and away at one school or another most of his days. He went to day school, and to grammar school, then to a Scottish public school. Then he went to the University of Edinbro', and after that to various universities here and there about the face of Europe. While he was away getting all this schooling his mother and father got older and older, and at last they got so old they died of it, both satisfied that they'd done their best for their son.

By that time he'd got all the knowledge he thought he needed, and he decided it was time to come home to the house his parents had left him and write a book about all the things he'd learned.

So back he came and settled into the house.

He found that it was a dreary old house in a dreary old street in the heart of the old part of Dundee, where the smoke from all the chimneys of the town had hung over it for long, long years. The Dundee Law seemed to tower over it and want to shut it in, although it was really not so near as it looked. But the house stood

close by the Howff, that ancient graveyard which has
held the honoured and famous dead of the town for
over three hundred years.

The house was as dark and dismal inside as it was
without. The walls were dark and damp and of no
sort of colour you could lay a name to. There were
great wooden shutters to the windows that kept the
light out, for his mother had always said the light would
fade the carpet.

Why he should stay there in the dank old place at
an age when other young men were out enjoying themselves was a queer sort of riddle. Maybe he couldn't
have told the answer to it himself, if he'd ever thought
about it at all.

There was no lack of money, for he'd been left
plenty. But he was a quiet, steady young man and his
wants were few, and maybe he was just glad to settle
down in peace after all the travelling around from one
school to another. So he took the house the way it was
and let it be.

His father and mother had never told him about the
bogles, and maybe they never noticed them at all, but
he soon found out about them for himself.

When he settled in he looked about till he found
himself a cook and a lass to keep house for him. The
two of them came with their boxes and took over.
But after they'd been there a day or two the cook
came to him and said, 'There's somewhat amiss with
the garret, maister.'

'What would it be?' he asked.

'The draughts is terrible,' she told him. 'Ye canna
keep a door ajar, but a breeze comes by and bangs it
shut. And the locks won't hold, for as soon as it's
shut the draught bangs it wide open again. What with

banging and creaking all the night the lass and me can get no sleep at all!'

'Well, move down to the next storey,' said the doctor. 'I'll have in a man to look to the garret.'

The man came and looked to the garret, but he could find naught wrong, for the windows were tight and he couldn't find the sign of a place for the draught to come in.

But a few days later the doctor came down to his breakfast to find the boxes of the two women in the hall and the women beside them, white as winding sheets.

The cook spoke for both of them. 'We'll be leaving ye, maister,' said she, 'this very morning's morn!'

'Why then?' asked the astonished doctor.

'We'll not be staying in a place where there's bogles!' said the cook firmly. The serving lass shrieked a wee shriek and rolled her eyes and clutched the cook's arm.

'Bogles!' The doctor laughed. 'You mean ghosts? Oh come, come now! You are a sensible woman. You know there are no such things as ghosts!'

'I know what I know!' said the cook.

Then the two of them picked up their boxes and out of the door they went, without waiting to ask could they get their wages!

Well, that was the way it was after that. The doctor would find himself a new couple of women to look after the house. They'd come with their boxes and all, but after a few days the boxes were down in the hall and the women beside them ready to go their ways, and all because of the bogles!

Two by two they came, and two by two they went, over and over again, and not even the promise of better wages would tempt them to stay.

And at last came a time when the doctor could find no one who would come at all, for the ones who left had spread the news wide and there wasn't a lass in the town of Dundee who'd step a foot into the doctor's house. No! Not even for all the money in Dundee!

Then the doctor took the ferry over the Tay to Newport, thinking maybe he could find a cook and housemaid there. But the news of the doctor's bogles had got to Newport before him, being the sort of news that travels fast. The Newport lassies who were willing to go into service would have nothing at all to do with him, after they found out who he was.

It came into his mind then that he'd heard that they had a wheen of ghosts in St Andrews. Maybe the women there'd be used to them, and wouldn't be minding a house that was said to have bogles in it.

Not that he believed in bogles himself. No indeed. Not he!

So he made the journey from Newport to St Andrews. But he had no luck there at all. There were bogles galore, 'tis true. In fact the place must have been teeming with them, for the folks at St Andrews told him proudly that there was scarcely a house in the town that hadn't a bogle or two in it — certainly not one of the older houses.

But the trouble with St Andrews was that if there was no lack of bogles, there were no lassies who weren't already in service. And they all said they were suited fine where they were, thank you, and wouldn't like to be making a change, even for the bigger wages the doctor was willing to pay.

So it looked as if he'd just have to do for himself, though he didn't know how to cook at all, and as for cleaning up and making things tidy he knew less about that.

He started back home again, for there was nothing else he could do.

When he was on the ferry going back from Newport to Dundee he saw a lass on the boat. She was the sort of a lass you look twice at, for she had the reddest hair in the world, springing up in wee curls in the fresh wind from the Tay. She had the white skin that goes with that sort of hair, and a saucy nose with a sprinkle of freckles across it, and eyes of the bluest blue he'd ever seen.

She was neat as a silver pin, too, with a little flat straw hat pinned tight to her curls and a white blouse and a tidy black skirt. But what he noticed most was her smile, for it was merry and kind.

He thought she wouldn't be minding if he went and spoke to her. So he went over and stood beside her at the rail of the boat.

'Do you believe in bogles?' he asked her.

She looked at him and her eyes crinkled, and she broke into a laugh. 'Och, do I not!' she cried. 'My old grannie at Blairgowrie that I'm going to stay with had a rare time with a pair of them a year or so back, till she rid them out!'

'Oh,' said he.

'Do you not believe in them?' asked the red-haired lass curiously.

'No, I don't!' said he.

And that was the end of that, for if she believed in bogles there was no use asking her to come and keep house for him, because she would not stay any more than the rest of them.

When he got back home he went into the scullery

to see what there was for his supper. But what was there that had to be cooked, he didn't know what to do with. He just had to make do with the heel of a loaf of bread and a bit of stale cheese that wasn't fit to bait a mousetrap with.

So when he went into his study he was hungry and he was tired and he was plain put about!

He sat down at his desk, and he banged his fist on it, and he shouted out loud, ' 'Tis all nonsense! THERE ARE NO BOGLES!'

'Oh, aren't there?' asked a quiet voice behind him.

He whirled round in his chair, and then his eyes popped out and his hair stood straight up on his head.

There were three big white things standing there, *and he could see right through them.*

But the doctor was awful stubborn. 'There are no bogles,' he said again, only his voice wasn't so loud this time and he didn't sound as if he was so sure about it.

'Then what would you be calling us?' asked one of them politely.

Well, there was no two ways about it. Bogles they were, and BOGLES he had to call them. So he had to admit that there *were* bogles in his house.

What he didn't know yet was how many of them were there. Because they liked his house fine. It was so nice and dark and damp.

It was not so bad as far as his meals went, for he was taking them at the inn, rather than starve at home. But at home he was fair distracted, for it seemed as if there were more and more bogles all the time.

Bogles peered down at him from over the rail of the staircase, and there were always some of them lurking about in the corners of any room he was in, blinking their eyes at him and sighing at him, and they fair gave him a chill. The three first ones followed him about, and when he went up to his bed at night they came along and sat on the foot of the bed and talked to him.

They all came from the Howff, they told him.

'Och, aye,' sighed one of them. ' 'Twas a fine grave-yard, one time.'

'For the first hundred years or so,' said the second bogle.

'But after that it began to get crowded. A lot of new people got brought in, and some of them wasn't the sort we'd want to neighbour with,' said the first one again.

But since they had found his place they told the doctor, 'twas far better. They liked it fine in his house, and all the best bogles were moving over there, too, so they felt much more at home than they did in the Howff.

Things being the way they were the doctor had no peace by day or by night. He was writing away on his learned book about some sort of wisdom or other, I wouldn't know what. He was having a hard time of it, for the bogles were that curious that they hung about him and peered over his shoulder, and even took to criticising what he wrote. One of them even got so familiar that he'd lean on the doctor's shoulder and point out places where the doctor could be doing better with his words. It annoyed the doctor a lot, because he found himself writing down what the bogle said, and he had ideas of his own that he liked better than the ones the bogle was giving him.

One day as he sat in the inn eating his dinner he

made up his mind that he'd take no more of the bogles, for he had had enough!

So he went home and put on his best clothes for a journey, and off he went to Blairgowrie to find the red-haired lass and ask her what her grannie had done to rid herself of her bogles.

When he got to Blairgowrie he went about the town looking for the lass. He couldn't ask for her for he didn't know her name. By and by he got to the end of the town and there he saw a neat little two-storey cottage, with a low stone wall around it, and inside the wall a big garden full of flowers. There was a bench by the door of the cottage, and on the bench sat the red-haired lass, and she was still smiling.

'Good day!' says he.

'Good day!' says she. 'I thought you'd soon be coming along.'

'You did!' said he, surprised. 'Why did you then?'

'Because you asked if I believed in bogles. So then I knew that you had some of your own and would be coming to find out what my grannie did to get rid of hers.'

He was amazed that one so bonny could be so wise. So he opened the gate and went into the garden. He sat down on the bench beside her and told her all his trouble.

'Will you come and help me get them out of the house?' he asked, when he'd finished his story.

'Of course I will!' said she.

Then she took him in to her grannie. Her grannie was just like her, only her hair was white and she wasn't so young, but her eyes were just as blue and her smile was as merry and kind.

'Grannie,' said the lass, 'I'm going with this gentleman to keep house for him, and to rid him of some bogles he has at home.'

'If anyone can, you can!' said her grannie, and the two of them laughed as if bogles were no trouble at all.

So the lass got ready and off she went with the doctor.

When he opened the door of his house and they went in, the lass wrinkled her nose and made a face. 'Faugh!' said she. 'It smells of bogle! A proper grave-yard smell,' she added, looking round at the place.

'They come from the Howff,' he told her, as if that explained it.

'I'll be bound!' she said. 'And to the Howff they'll go back!'

That night the doctor ate his meal at home, instead of going to the inn. It was a good one, too, for the lass got it, and nobody had ever said that she didn't know how to cook.

There wasn't a sign of a bogle that night, but that was because they were biding their time and looking the lass over.

The next morning the lass came into the study. She had on a blue overall, the same colour as her eyes, and there was a fresh white kerchief tied to cover her hair.

'This is a proper dark old place,' said she, looking about the room. 'Why do you not throw back those big old shutters and open the windows to let a wee bit of sun and fresh air in?'

'My mother said it would let dust in and fade the carpets,' the doctor said. He remembered that from the time when he was a wee lad, before he went off to his schools.

'What if it does!' said she. 'Can you not buy new ones?'

'I never thought of that!' he said. 'Of course I can.'

So the lass pulled the curtains back and folded back the wooden shutters. Then she opened the windows wide and the sea air came pouring in from the harbour, with the sun riding on top of it.

'That's better!' the lass told him.

'It is, indeed!' said the doctor, as he took a long, deep breath of the fresh cool air.

But the red-haired lass took another look at the dingy old room and frowned. 'No wonder you have bogles,' she said. 'I never saw a place they'd like better. But I can do no more for you till time for your dinner, so I'll leave you. I'm turning out the scullery.'

So the doctor worked at his book and the lass worked at the scullery, and the day went by.

That night the bogles came in a crowd and gathered round the doctor's bed.

'Who is the red-haired lass in the house?' asked the first bogle.

'She's my new housekeeper,' the doctor told them, yawning because he had worked awful hard on his learned book all day. The bogles hadn't come near him, because they didn't like all the sunlight that came into the study after the lass opened the windows.

'Is she going to stay here?' they asked.

'I hope so!' yawned the doctor. He had had a good supper, and he'd eaten a lot of it, and now he was so sleepy he couldn't keep his eyes open. Before the bogles had time to ask him anything else he'd fallen fast asleep.

They couldn't wake him for all they tried. So they gave him up and went to see could they scare the red-haired lass away, the same as they had the others. But she had worked hard and eaten well, too, so they couldn't waken her, no more than they could the doctor. They all agreed it was a bad day for the bogles when the lass came into the house. It was going to take an awful lot of hard work to get her out again.

The next day the red-haired lass was up early, and the day after that, and the next day after, too. The kitchen and the scullery were beginning to look like different places, for she swept and dusted and scrubbed and scoured and polished from morn to night. The doctor saw little of her except at mealtimes, but the meals were the best he'd ever had in his life, and she sat across the table from him and poured his tea and smiled at him.

At night he and the lass were so tired out, him with his writing and her with her turning out, that they couldn't be bothered about the bogles.

The bogles were there, nonetheless. They'd brought a lot more bogles from the Howff to help them — even some of the riff-raff they'd moved to the doctor's house to get away from! There were plenty of dark old rooms in the house still, for the lass was still busy with the scullery and the kitchen and hadn't come off the ground floor yet.

So at night the bogles tried all their best tricks that never had failed before. They swept through the house like a tempest, banging doors open and shut, wailing and gibbering, moaning and mowing, clanking chains and rattling bones, and the like.

It all did no good. Nobody heard them except maybe a passer-by in the street, who thought it was the wind rising from the sea, and hurried home so as not to get caught in a storm.

When the end of the week came along the red-haired lass said to the doctor, 'You'd best take your pens and paper and things over to my grannie's at Blairgowrie and do your writing there. I'm through with the kitchen and the scullery, and now I'm going to turn out the rest of the house.'

He didn't want to go, but she told him he'd got to for he'd only be in her way.

'You can leave me some money to get some things I'll be needing, and to pay for help to come in, to do what I can't do myself,' she told him. 'And don't come back till I send for you, mind!'

So he packed up, and off he went to her grannie's house as she told him to.

As soon as he was gone, the red-haired lass started in again, and now she really showed what she could do. The bogles were so upset about what was going on that one night they laid in wait for her and caught her on the stairs as she was going up to her bed. They tried to look as grisly as they could, and the noises they made were something horrible.

But the red-haired lass only stared straight through them. 'Go away, you nasty things!' she said.

'We won't then!' they said indignantly. 'We got here first and we've a mind to stay. Why don't you go away?'

'I like my work and I'm useful here,' said the lass. 'Which is more than you can say.'

'It was all fine till you came,' complained one of the bogles.

'It was all wrong till I came,' said the lass right back at them. 'And I wish you'd stop argy-bargying and let me get to my bed. I've a big day's work ahead of me tomorrow, for the painters are coming in and the men to take away the shutters, and when they're done 'twill be all sunny and bright and a treat to see!'

All the bogles groaned like one big groan.

'Sunny!' moaned one.

'Bright!' shrieked another.

'Well anyway, we're not going away,' said they.

'Stay if you like,' said the lass. 'It's all one to me if you stay or go. But you won't like it!' she promised them. And with that she walked straight up the steps and through the lot of them, and went to bed and to sleep.

After that the battle between the bogles and the lass really began. You couldn't say they didn't put up a fight for it, but the lass was more than a match for them. She drove them from the first storey of the house to the second, and from the second to the third, and from the third to the garret, for they couldn't stand the sunlight and brightness that followed her as she went up through the house at her work.

At last they had to pack up their extra winding sheets and their chains and bones and things and go back to the graveyard they'd come from, for the house wasn't fit for a bogle to stay in, and even if the Howff was crowded it suited them better now.

Well, when the painters and carpenters and all were gone the lass found a serving-maid to help her with the work. And this one stayed! But the lass didn't bother to look for a cook, for she thought her own cooking would suit the doctor best when he came back to his house.

The doctor was just as comfortable in her grannie's house and just as well fed there, and everything was fine, except that he missed the red-haired lass, for he'd begun to get used to having her around. There were no bogles to bother him at the lass's grannie's house, for she had rid herself of hers a long time ago. It came to his mind that he hadn't seen much of his own bogles lately, but he didn't miss them at all.

A week went by and then a second one and a third one. And the doctor found that instead of writing his learned book he'd be sitting and thinking how bright the red-haired lass's hair looked with the sun on it or how blue her eyes were or how the freckles looked on her saucy little nose. He was that homesick for her, he'd even have put up with the bogles, just to be at home, with her pouring out his tea and smiling at him across the table.

So when she sent word at the end of the fourth week that he was to come back he went off so fast that he almost forgot to thank her grannie for having him and to say good-bye!

When he got back to his house he had to step out into the road and look well at it, for he wasn't sure it was his.

The windows were open from ground floor to garret, and all the heavy wooden shutters had been taken away entirely. There were fresh white curtains blowing gently at all the windows and flowerpots on the sills.

Then the door opened and the red-haired lass stood in the doorway and smiled at him. It was his house after all!

'You've come then!' said she.

'I've come!' said he. And up the steps he went, two at a time. He could hardly believe 'twas the same place, when he saw what she'd done with it. Everything was light and bright, and through the whole house the fresh sea air blew, in one window and out another, so that the place was as sweet and fresh and wholesome as the red-haired lass herself.

'How about the bogles?' asked the doctor.

'They're gone,' said the lass.

'All of them? Where did they go?' asked the doctor.

'Back to the Howff, I suppose,' said the lass. 'This isn't the sort of place bogles would be liking to bide in.'

'No!' said the doctor, looking around. 'I can see that for myself.'

But he had one more question to ask, so he asked it. 'Will you marry me?' he said.

'Of course I will!' said the red-haired lass. And she smiled at him and said, 'Why else did you think I came here in the first place?'

So they were married, and the doctor had no more bogles in his house. But what he did have was half a dozen bairns, lads and lassies, all with red hair and blue eyes and saucy noses with freckles across them and merry smiles, just like their mother.

And bairns are better to fill a house with than bogles ever could be, so they all lived merrily ever after.